£2.49

20

CW00502559

# The Notary

# ALEXANDROS RANGAVIS

# The Notary

Translated by
Simon Darragh

AIORA

Simon Darragh has translated among other things the works of Nikos Kavvadias, and Andreas Laskaratos's *Reflections* (Aiora 2015). *Foreign Correspondence* (Peterloo 2000) is a volume of Darragh's own poetry. Simon Darragh has been a Hawthornden Fellow, and a Translator in Residence at the University of East Anglia. He now lives noisily in the Northern Sporades.

*This book was published with the support of the Kostas and Helen Ouranis Foundation.*

Original title: *Ὁ συμβολαιογράφος*

ISBN: 978-618-5048-66-2

First edition March 2017
Reprinted October 2022

AIORA PRESS
11 Mavromichali St.
Athens 10679 - Greece
tel: +30 210 3839000
www.aiora.gr

This story is set in the early 1820s on Cephalonia, one of the seven Ionian Islands in western Greece (Corfu, Paxos, Lefkas, Cephalonia, Ithaca, Zante, Kythira). At that time, the modern Greek state did not exist; the decline of the Byzantine Empire had led to the gradual occupation of most of the Greek-speaking world by the Ottoman Turks by the end of the fifteenth century. The Ionian Islands remained the only part of what we now know as Greece that was never under Ottoman control. For nearly six hundred years, starting in the thirteenth century, the islands were under the rule of the Republic of Venice, which left them with a blend of Greek and Italian language and culture. In 1797, the islands transferred to French rule with Napoleon's conquest of Venice. In 1809, the British defeated the French in the Ionian, and the islands became a British protectorate as of 1815. After the Greek Revolution in 1821 and the establishment of an independent Greek state on the mainland a few years later, the Ionian Islands petitioned for incorporation, eventually joining Greece in 1864.

# Contents

# I

Those Greeks who enjoyed the enthusiastic hospitality of the Cephalonians in the early days of the Revolution may remember the notary Tapas, of Argostoli, the island's capital: a wrinkled old man, stooping, bald, with a toothy grin and a sidelong glance hidden behind green-tinted glasses. His speech was—as throughout the Ionian Islands in those days—an adulterated mixture of Greek and Italian, remaining from the Venetian dynasty.*

Well, one day towards evening Mr Tapas was sitting on a rickety stool at his desk, writing, not taking much notice of the many customers waiting their turn, when, with a youthful hesitant step, someone came through the door and approached him. Tapas peered furtively over his glasses. Recognizing his visitor, he pushed his glasses onto his forehead, tucked his pen behind his ear, and called him over in his usual dialect, heavily larded with Italian, the entirety of which we refrained from reproducing in this text:

'So it's yourself, Signor Rodini! Welcome, *mia gioia*.[1] What is Signor Count Nannetos's command?'

'The count, unfortunately, is still unwell,' the young man replied, speaking correct Greek. 'And I come not on his behalf, but on my own, to beg a personal favour.'

The notary automatically lowered his glasses, as the word 'favour' had frightened him, and however carefully he might control his tongue, he didn't want his eyes to betray him.

'Oh, *bene, bene!*'[2] he said. 'What d'you need? Tell me!'

'My plans may well require as much as a thousand *distila*;[3] I should like to know if you are in a position to advance me such a sum.'

The notary gave his habitual vulpine laugh.

'A thousand *distila*!' he said. 'Signor, my son, money doesn't grow on trees in Cephalonia these days. Business is failing, *caro*;[4] the price of raisins has fallen, and the coffers are empty.'

'Mr Tapas,' said Rodini, 'I am aware of the problems, so I came to you in advance as I shall only need the loan in a few days, if at all. To ease matters fur-

---

1. 'My joy'
2. 'Good, good!'
3. Spanish eight-reales coin, a widely used trading currency
4. 'Dear'

ther, I should like you to know that, in the matter of interest and so on, you have no need to be gentle with me: I am ready for any sacrifice.'

'*Va bene, va bene!*[5] But as I say, times are hard, *caro*. These days, whoever has a penny keeps it, or, if he *does* lend it, he wants very strong security.'

'I give you my signature!' said Rodini, much as a Spanish Grandee might say, 'I give my moustache as security!'

'Your signature, Signor Rodini! If it were up to me, *carissimo*,[6] I'd give you the wealth of Croesus if I had it. But the money-lenders, unfortunately, are not content with reputation.'

'Well, they can hold back the wages Count Nan-netos pays me. Won't that satisfy them?'

'Oh, as to that, why shouldn't it satisfy them? But you know what those bad people say? "Wages are here today and gone tomorrow." And anyway, let's say your wages cover the interest. What about the capital?'

'God will provide, my dear sir: the capital shall be found,' Rodini replied cheerfully.

'Well, God…' said Tapas, shrugging his shoulders. 'But you see, my boy, God is not obliged to pay on the money-lenders' terms. Believe me, *caro mio*, a loan is a

---

5. 'Alright, alright!'
6. 'Dearest'

rotten foundation. It's a millstone round your neck and it will take you to the bottom. Keep away from loans; mark my words: you don't fly far on borrowed wings.'

'Look, my dear notary; if you find me the thousand *distila*,' Rodini replied, in the manner of one needing money rather than advice, 'and if the lender is not satisfied with my wages, you can tell him that he can have actual property as security.'

'Your house in Corfu? *Mi dispiace*,[7] but you wouldn't get two hundred *distila* for that.'

'Well if even that won't do,' said Rodini, 'you can offer my house, garden, fields, and vineyards here in Cephalonia; property that's worth ten times the loan.'

The notary turned to Rodini in astonishment, as if he thought he must be mad, and looked him up and down from head to toe. Rodini came closer and spoke in low tones:

'Mr Tapas, could I have a few words in private?'

'*Va bene*, dear sirs,' said the notary, addressing his other customers, 'we'll discuss your business tomorrow. *Arrivederci*,[8] gentlemen.'

With smiles and gestures he gave them to understand his meaning, namely, 'For the moment, do me the favour of clearing off.'

---

7. 'I am sorry'
8. 'Goodbye'

The customers got the idea, and in a few moments only Rodini remained in front of the notary.

'So, we have palaces and castles, *caro amico*.[9] We are millionaires. And might I ask, pray,'—this with a sharp, piercing look, while feigning a lack of curiosity—'how this miracle occurred? If you've found some buried treasure, what d'you want with a loan, I wonder?'

'My dear Mr Tapas,' said Rodini, 'a notary is like a confessor, in whom one can safely confide. I can tell you things that shouldn't be heard by all those others. To begin with, it would be pointless to tell you right now what I want with a loan. In some days, you may well receive an invitation to a ceremony, which will explain why I must, without fail, have cash.'

'Oh, oh! *Capisco*![10] *Per Dio*![11] Congratulations, Signor Rodini! There's a whiff of matrimony about this business, by Bacchus! And are we permitted to know...'

'You will know, my dear sir, when the time comes.'

'Ah, good heavens! A secret marriage! So that's it! And a big fat dowry? Ah, so *that's* where the castles and vineyards... But, *caro*, don't you know that a dowry can't be given as material security?'

---

9. "Dear friend'
10. 'I understand'
11. 'By God!'

'I know, Mr Tapas, but the security I offer is not a dowry.'

Leaning closer to the notary and looking round to make sure he wouldn't be overheard, he said:

'The security I offer is the estate of Count Nannetos. He has made me his sole heir. That, I hope, should be enough for even the most difficult of lenders.'

'What? What? His heir?' the notary exclaimed, shooting up from his stool as if on springs, then adjusting his spectacles and half-closing his eyes in the way a cat does when it wants to show indifference. '*Per Dio Santo,*'[12] he continued, 'the count has made you his heir? *Bello*, oh *bello*![13] But, *carissimo*, are you quite sure? *I* don't remember writing any such testament.'

'No, Mr Tapas; the will was made in private.'

'Oh? And when was that, might I ask?'

'Today, just now. But understand, I don't want it made known.'

'*Per Dio*, who d'you think you're talking to? Count Nannetos's heir! By Saint Yerasimos,[14] that's solid security! But just a moment, just a moment, *carissimo*: the count has a nephew, has he not?'

'Yerasimos of Lixouri is his nephew.'

'Well, and isn't *he* the sole heir?'

---

12. 'Holy God'
13. 'Nice, oh nice!'

'He ought to be,' Rodini replied, 'and, believe me, Mr Tapas, I did everything possible to change the uncle's mind, but in vain. I saw I was only distressing him, without achieving anything. I was even ready to provoke his anger by not accepting. "Don't deny me," he said, "and don't so much as mention my nephew's name to me. He's always been the dark cloud in my life; may he be far from my death-bed! Don't have any pangs of conscience; accede to my wishes: I give *you* my inheritance so that through you it will go to him to whom it a hundredfold belongs; to the man who would never accept anything directly from my hands. Through you I give it to the man who was the victim of my worthless nephew's theft: I give it to him who has, in heroic friendship, remained poor and without honour rather than distress me by exposing my relative's shame. You don't want to accept my riches? But wouldn't you at least help me to die in the felicity of having done my duty before God?"—you see, then, that it was impossible for me to refuse.'

'*Per Dio*! And Count Yerasimos…?'

'He's disinherited his nephew Yerasimos, and put a curse against me in his will if I give Yerasimos any part of the inheritance.'

---

14. The patron saint of Cephalonia

'Disinherited!' said Tapas with a spasmodic laugh, jumping up from his seat. 'Disinherited! Oh, *bella cosa*![15] But I must advise you, *caro* Rodini: take care not to get involved in a lot of complications. No one can cut their legal heirs out of their will without valid reason. Count Yerasimos might seek the decision of the courts.'

'Unfortunately,' Rodini replied, 'there's no shortage of reasons, and to make sure, he mentioned them in the will. That's why he drew it up privately, you see.'

'Of course, of course. I, too, have heard about the youthful indiscretions of Count Yerasimos. But that Count Dionysios Nannetos—who's considered a second saint here—would be so angry I can't believe it.'

'It's not for me to judge,' said Rodini, 'but you shouldn't think Count Dionysios's conduct reprehensible. Yerasimos dishonoured the name of Nannetos: he was imprisoned for theft in Italy. The shame of that was like an arrow in his uncle's heart; it drove him to his sickbed, it will drive him to his grave. But having compassion, and being moved by Yerasimos's letters, all of which showed repentance, the count disregarded his conduct as a young man's foolishness, rescued him from prison, and covered up his dishonour. The count's circle all accepted Yerasimos without

---

15. 'A nice thing!'

suspicion, and that rich merchant Ioannis Voratis, who had been the benefactor of Count Dionysios in former times and later became his bosom friend, befriended Yerasimos; a very son of the family. But one day Voratis went to Corfu, leaving Yerasimos at his premises. When he came back, Yerasimos had gone off on some journey and thieves had broken into Voratis's treasury. The theft bankrupted him; the rich man was reduced to destitution. You remember, perhaps, how surprised people were when, instead of making haste to discover the culprit, the victim on the contrary abandoned the pursuit, so that suspicions arose that the bankruptcy was fraudulent. Voratis saw his reputation destroyed and his family descend into poverty, and put up with all this rather than break the heart of his sick and aged friend Count Dionysios Nannetos. And from that time, the count's illness took on a fatal character. But Count Dionysios knows the perpetrator, and understands the silent devotion of Voratis. Count Dionysios has expelled his nephew from his heart, and would like to reward Voratis indirectly.

'Now that you have understood me, my dear Mr Tapas, see if you can advance me the loan, should I ask for it in some days.'

Rodini was silent now, but so too was the notary, who cupped his head in his hands and sank deep into thought. During their silence, a guitar could be heard in the next room, and two voices singing:

*The envious moon will hide...*

Finally Tapas, as if waking from a deep sleep, looked around him with an air of astonishment, and saw Rodini:

'Ah, *caro mio*,' he said, collecting his thoughts, 'the loan, right? The loan? *Va bene, va bene.* We'll talk tomorrow and put things straight. This evening, *con permesso*,[16] I have a few things to do. Tomorrow, *carissimo* Signor Rodini.'

And so saying he got up. Rodini did the same; they made their farewells and Rodini left.

'My respects to Signor the Count,' Tapas called. '*Arrivederci.*'[17]

And silently added:

'Go to the Devil.'

Afterwards, Tapas went to the door of the adjoining room and opened it with a kick.

---

16. 'With your permission'
17. 'Goodbye'

## II

The notary stood on the threshold with his arms folded. He had lifted his spectacles, those telegraphs of his feelings, onto his forehead, exposing the two people sitting on the balcony to the lightning flashes of his gaze.

A lovely young girl, blue-eyed and blonde haired, with a melancholy facial expression, was singing with a sweet voice and making big, loving eyes at a young man half-reclining beside her as he accompanied her with both voice and guitar.

'What d'you think, *cara*, of that G-sharp?' he said, stopping his strumming. 'I learnt it from Tambourini. The top Prima Donna at the San Carlos theatre in Naples quite lost her mind when she heard it, and since then she knows me by no other name than "Mr G-sharp".'

At that moment he noticed the notary standing in the darkness of the doorway.

'Ah, good evening, Signor Tapas. What a pity you weren't in time to hear my famous G-sharp. But this evening you were obliged to work late.'

'Your Honour has turned up very early,' the old man replied sullenly.

'Early, he says? The old father is witty. And d'you know where I've come from? Straight from Corfu, by the direct route! You shrug your shoulders? But, by St Yerasimos, I'm telling the truth. Two months ago I ordered a superb horse from Malta, and I bet Major Redcoat and his officers I could race them from Lixouri to Faraklata and get there at least five minutes before the others. If I lost, I'd have to stand dinner for all the officers, wherever they were. Ten days ago they brought me the mare; I paid 800 shillings for her… or I will when I can get it. You should see her, old man; she's so beautiful you'll want to kiss her on the mouth. We raced the day before yesterday, and the happy creature flew like the wind. But somewhere near the village, I don't know what came over her, she reared up and threw me. Then the Petty Officer Horsewhip overtook me… if the officers hadn't stopped me, I'd have drawn my pistol and blown her brains out. So yesterday I gave the dinner, at Mount Ainos: that's why you didn't see me yesterday evening. Old man Tapas, you who know history, the Ionian Islands haven't witnessed such a dinner since the Phaeacians treated Odysseus. We drank a Tokay wine undreamt of even in the Hungarian Court.'

'And good health to you,' Tapas said sarcastically.

'And that's nothing,' Yerasimos continued, 'Major Redcoat, like some of his officers, is stationed in Corfu. Well I owed them a dinner too. So I chartered a schooner and loaded it with food and wine, and I had it wait for us ready to anchor off Mount Ainos, where we ate. When the party was over I said goodbye to my friends and went on board, and we set sail. I hadn't seen Marina two days before, nor said goodbye to her. So what did I do? When the boat had signalled goodbye to the officers and turned its prow towards Corfu, I boarded the launch —without the officers seeing me, because it was already almost dark—and went back to Argostoli. Before dawn I'll be out on the open seas again. My dinner will be a sensation, old man. All the newspapers in the Ionian Islands would talk about it—if the Ionian Islands had newspapers. The Naples papers talked for a month about the breakfast I gave in Pompeii because I'd had a bet with an Englishman about whether the brightness of the second singer's face was natural, like the sun's, or borrowed, like the moon's.

'Marina, my girl, go and see about dinner,' said Tapas, and when the young woman had left he turned to Yerasimos and said, 'So you enjoyed yourself in Naples, Signor Count?'

'Listen to that! I had a great life!'

'And since you had such a great life, tell me, pray, why did you abandon it?'

So saying, the notary stretched his thin lips in a sardonic smile.

'I left, Mr Tapas, I left… how can I explain? I left because my principles didn't quite match the principles of the Neapolitan kingdom's police. I was of a liberal turn of mind there, and the ministers were suspicious of me. They wanted to imprison me as a *carbonaro*.[18] Imprison me! Your humble servant! Well I got out of the cage and flew back to my nest.'

'Well done, Signor Count! And tell me, why didn't you stay in your nest and hatch your eggs? Your spirit took you in another direction again? And you know what else? Just when you left, they broke into poor Voratis's strong-box and stole his entire livelihood, leaving him totally helpless. Did you hear about that, Signor Count?'

'And what if I did hear about it?' said the count impatiently. 'Am I the keeper of Signor Voratis's cash-box?'

---

18. *Carbonari*: members of secret revolutionary societies from the early nineteenth century in the Kindgdom of Naples.

'Oh, well said, well said, Signor Count! That's an old story. That's what Cain said once about his brother. But tell me, *caro*, what are your plans now? You went to Naples, and they threw you into prison because you were a freedom-lover. You came back, then left again, I don't know why, just when they robbed Signor Voratis…'

'What? What's that supposed to mean?' shouted Yerasimos angrily.

'How should I know what it means? Don't worry; it's past and forgotten! But now, just tell me this: what do you plan to do?'

'You know very well. When the old man fades away, I'll take my Marina and we'll go straight to Rome. And from there to Paris, then London, to enjoy the world, just as the lords enjoy it. Then I'll come back here and build two palaces, then I'll buy a yacht, then I'll get six horses, and then from time to time I'll invite My Lord the British Governor to my dinners.'

'You'll do golden works, Signor Yerasimos. But I'll just advise you of one thing: you'll do all this *before* you take my daughter.'

'But why, old man?'

'For one very simple reason: because you'll *never* take my daughter.'

'What are you saying?' shouted Yerasimos hurriedly. 'Why shan't I take her?'

'Because I shan't give her to you.'

'Are you joking, Father-in-Law? Won't you explain?'

'You want me to explain? *Benissimo*![19] Now listen! You're in such a hurry to have Marina because you know she's rich.'

'Oh!' the count replied.

'None of your "Oh's!" Listen to what I have to say.' The notary continued: 'As long as old Tapas lives —and, by Bacchus, I hope you won't have the trouble of burying him yourself—he wants his possessions for himself.'

'But do you suppose,' muttered Yerasimos, 'that I seek Marina for her riches? No; I want her for her beauty; for her virtues.'

'Signor Count, did you learn diplomacy in the Naples prison?' asked the old man mercilessly. 'I do believe you love her. If I didn't believe that, it would never have crossed my mind to let you have her. But love doesn't bring home the bacon. And I'd die before I'd let my daughter beg for bread with her husband.'

'Beg for bread with her husband, old man?' said Yerasimos, laughing proudly. 'That's rich! D'you imagine the count, my uncle, is made of iron, or has drunk the elixir of life? Tomorrow, or the next day, he'll sleep in peace. Then you won't call me a beggar.'

---

19. 'Very good!'

'If the signor, your uncle, dies, it's you who'll be paying for the burial.'

'Don't worry, old Tapas: I'll pay, and handsomely. I'll pay out of the inheritance, and what he'll be leaving is millions.'

'*Mio caro*, in your dreams: your inheritance is an empty shell.'

'What! You're not even satisfied with my inheritance? You're being difficult, by Saint Yerasimos.'

'It's taken wing, your inheritance: it's flown the coop, I tell you; don't you understand?'

'Taken wing? Where to?' asked Yerasimos, seeming not to know whether the old man was serious or joking.

'It's flown to the bosom of Rodini. D'you understand now?'

'What does that mean? You're talking in riddles, old Tapas,' said the young man, quite astonished.

'I'm telling you loud and clear,' said the notary, 'that Count Nannetos has disinherited your good self, and left his fortune to Rodini.'

'Ha, ha!' went the young man. 'Fairy tales, Father! Old Methuselah has disinherited *me*, the support, glory, and hope of his family?'

'It's no fairy tale, *caro*; I'm telling you the plain truth. It made a bad impression on him that you were a 'liberal' and a *carbonaro* in Naples, and didn't stay to look after Signor Voratis's treasury. You see, old Methuselah has his own ideas.'

'Well, then what are you telling me?'

'I'm telling you that you can wipe your uncle's inheritance from your account book once and for all. He made a special private will and he hasn't left you a button, Signor Count.'

'Tapas! Tapas, old man! If you haven't gone back to infancy, old Father; if you haven't lost your reason, you'll make me lose mine!' Yerasimos burst out angrily. 'The old man did that to me? Disinherited me, the old sod? I'll suck his blood, by Saint Yerasimos!—Tapas, I'm up to my ears in debt. He's stealing my inheritance, he's stealing my very self, taking, just think, my life and my breath! I'll go to court!'

'Go ahead, Signor Count; then you'll have to pay the expenses of the case.'

'So what should I do?'

'What should you do? *Per Dio*! You should go, oh grand defender of liberty!, you should go to Naples,

*And fill the cannon's belly*
*with Italian Vermicelli!'*

'I swear to you, Tapas old man, I'll take a knife and kill myself.'

'That would be a golden piece of work, by Bacchus. Rodini will write your epitaph.'

'Are you sure? If my uncle dies in this frame of mind…'

'If the signor your uncle dies, and the will remains as it is, I'm quite certain that Rodini will inherit, come what may.'

'I must act in time, then. The old man's been in the throes of death for six months now; I'd say he has seven souls; his soul must be wedged deep in his very bones. I'm afraid, Tapas, he might die before I can manage matters. Now, Tapas, I want him to live.'

'Well, well! Now you're talking like a good nephew,' said the old man ironically. 'Long live Uncle!'

'And if this will exists, isn't there some way to revoke it?' asked the count, racking his brains, in his unhappiness turning and torturing himself in all directions.

'Isn't there some way, you say?' the cunning old man answered with insistent mockery. 'Signor Uncle only has to call for me and tell me, "Write this, write that," and then sign it personally, and indeed it is revoked.'

'To call for you and tell you… No, that's impossible!' said Yerasimos hopelessly. 'He could never be persuaded to do that! I know; I mean it!'

And he strode up and down the room.

'But…' he continued after a short silence, 'if, instead of his calling you, I were to take him a draft, already written, and he were to sign it, wouldn't that be valid? Isn't it the same?'

'Well it's not the same, but it might help.'

'Then write, Tapas, write whatever's necessary.'

'Ah, but what's the point? Would he ever sign it for you?'

'Write, write, I say. I'll think about it; we'll see later.'

'Writing isn't the difficulty,' said the notary, shaking his head and throwing a sharp look at Yerasimos.

After he'd been writing some time, he read out the following in a loud voice:

'Before me, public notary in Argostoli, capital of Cephalonia, and the witnesses Nikolos Vaphouras and Dionysis Servetas, known to me, and having no family relation to me...'

'Ah! Witnesses!' said Yerasimos, blanching. 'The witnesses will have to sign too!'

'You make sure your uncle signs and don't worry about the witnesses. They're good, honourable men. I've got them out of trouble three times, and when they sign for me, their left hands don't know what their right hands are doing.'

And he carried on reading:

'... Signor Count Dionysios Nannetos has declared as follows: Being aware that he is on the point of death, he states that his sole heir and legatee, legally and incontestably, to all his mobile and immobile possessions is his beloved nephew Count Yerasimos Nannetos. And this being his sole and irrevocable wish, he lets it be known to all and sundry that he has never made any other testament, public or private, anterior to this. And that any other that may be found posteriorly, unless it be a codicil to this testament, is false and invalid.—Made in Argostoli, capital of Cephalonia…'

'I've dated it one month ago,' continued the notary. 'All is in order, Signor Count. Here's your inheritance! You're a millionaire, *caro*. Pity there's one little word missing at the end. Go and be nice, stroke him, baby your signor uncle. If he writes that little word for you, I give you my compliments. If he doesn't—take the Naples boat.'

'He'll write it, Tapas,' roared Yerasimos. 'By fair means or foul, he must write it.'

'By foul, he says! Oh, *bello*! Wise counsel you're croaking, *per Dio*!' replied the old man with an ugly look. 'And if he signs it by foul means, don't you realize he only has to live two more minutes, and say one more little word, to send you not to the Naples prison, but straight to the gallows, Signor Count, *carissimo*?'

'And if I send it to you signed,' asked Yerasimos after a moment's silence, 'are you ready to carry it through?'

'Send it,' said Tapas, 'and I shall make sure they respect the signor count's reputation and his last wishes.'

'Give it to me, then, give it!' shouted the young man. 'And with God's help… or the Devil's!'

And as he left, standing on the threshold:

'Bear in mind, old Tapas, that whatever you do for me, you do for Marina.'

And he dashed out of the door.

'Oh, I bear it in mind, I bear it in mind,' whispered Tapas when he was alone. 'If I didn't bear it in mind, would I have put my neck in the noose for your fine black eyes, my son?'

A moment later the notary's daughter came skipping into the room and called gaily:

'To dinner, gentlemen, to dinner!'

But then she stood motionless in the middle of the room, gazed about in astonishment with her big blue eyes, and asked:

'But where's Yerasimos?'

'He's gone,' said her father. 'He won't be dining with us tonight.'

'He won't be dining with us?' she said in altered tones. 'And I told him I'd picked the cherries from our tree myself!'

'And you can't help but cry,' said her father, stroking her gently, 'because he won't be eating your cherries! You're such a child! He had something urgent to do, and left.'

'So very urgent that he couldn't even wish us goodnight?' and it looked as if she really would burst into tears.

'Child,' said Tapas, 'do you really love that Yerasimos so much?'

Without answering, Marina took her father's hand and kissed it, thus hiding her flaming cheeks.

'Never mind, my girl, never mind,' said Tapas, 'I won't be cross with you; love him, *per Dio*! Since you want him, take him! When he inherits from his uncle, you'll be the richest and most envied woman in the Ionian Islands.'

Then Marina wrapped her arms about her father's neck, and her tears flowed freely. The notary enfolded the happy girl in his embrace, and kissed her forehead with more strength and feeling than one might have expected, knowing the dry and twisted character of the old man. But, just as in the middle of an arid plain or on the edge of a storm-blasted precipice one tree thrives in isolation, a reminder of luxuriant forests, and its vitality, fed on the vitality of the remainder, comes as a surprise, so too it can happen, in a heart hardened or in the grip of the vilest vice, that a sole noble feeling may survive and thrive all the more impressively. Such, in Tapas's heart, was affection.

As a young man he had married, against her parents' wishes, the daughter of one of the island's most important and richest merchants. This was his first and last youthful indiscretion, in which, though, his mind was no indifferent spectator of the agitations of his youthful heart. His wife had died giving birth to Marina, who remained for him a reminder of his short-lived happiness and a signal to others of his triumphant selfishness.

Consequently, he concentrated on her the power of every trace of love left in his heart, and this feeling grew so strong that it absorbed not only the few drops of nobility that can still be found in the most corrupt souls, but fed, too, on his soul's sickest juices, and had the combined force of both virtue and fault.

In fact, he wouldn't hesitate to make any sacrifice, however great, or to commit any crime, however abhorrent, if by such means he could buy his daughter riches, enjoyment, happiness.

# III

After leaving the notary, Rodini went to the town centre, to a winding street, and entered a clean, respectable but unostentatious house. At the top of the stairs he happened to meet a young woman watering flowers in pots, who might herself have been taken for a sister to the flowers. Her figure was slimmer than most of the local girls'; the hands with which, like an archaic nymph, she held the silver watering-can, were whiter than jasmine, and her smiling lips were redder than carnations. This was Angeliki, the daughter of Augustin Voratis.

It should be admitted that Rodini's fortunate chance encounter occurred almost every afternoon, and he would lose himself, as it were, for one or even two hours at the head of the stairs in this prologue to his regular visits to Mr Voratis and Angeliki; for the two young people loved each other as might two sibling souls, though they had not admitted as much to each other, or even to themselves.

Their feelings, however—clear and genuine—
had not escaped the eye of Mr Voratis. But the idea of
their union, for all that in his heart he might wish
it, didn't cross his mind, or, if it did, it was a source of
sadness to him, because the fact that they were both
poor was an inescapable obstacle to its realization.
As for Rodini, rare were the moments he saw this un-
realizable vision, a golden but impossible daydream,
of which he had said not a word to Angeliki.

'Hurry, Mr Rodini,' she called as she saw him
coming up the stairs, 'come and see: the Bengal rose
you gave me has bloomed, and it would be ungrateful
of it not to after I gave it so much attention. Because,
Mr Rodini, I love Bengal roses… especially this one,'
she added gently and hesitantly as he reached her side.

But he, instead of replying, as he did on other
occasions to prolong his stay with her, this time took
her hand and raised it impulsively to his lips; something which he had never dared do as long as he'd
known her. And before the astonished young woman
had a chance to demand an explanation for this ef-
frontery, he left her and ran indoors to her father.

But Angeliki followed him on tiptoe, light as a
shadow, curious to find out—if it was permitted—
what so very important matter Rodini had to talk to
her father about, and concerning which he hadn't
said a word to her.

But Rodini had nothing special to say.

'Count Dionysios invites you,' he said, 'if you aren't busy this evening, to come to him for a little while, with Miss Angeliki, as he is unhappy on his own.'

He made this harmless invitation in such a troubled voice, however, that Angeliki couldn't help realizing that something must have happened today.

Anyway, it should be understood that his friend's wish was law for Voratis, so at once, bringing his daughter, he accompanied Rodini to the count's.

They found the old man confined to bed, as he had been for some time, brought down above all by the extreme bad behaviour of his nephew, his health having already been jeopardised by the sorrows of his earlier life. But from his face, for all that it was tortured by physical pain, shone the cheerful calm of a soul at peace, and his eyes filled with heartfelt joy when he saw his friends arriving.

'My beloved Voratis,' he said, 'thank you for coming with your dear daughter. The older I get, my friends, the more egoistic I become. My life is measured in moments, and I want to be warmed by your presence, just as others, when they are dying, want to see the sun.'

'Don't say such sad words, dear Count,' said Voratis. 'Fate will not for many years yet, I hope, be so envious of the happiness we feel by being together in this world.'

'Don't you believe it, my friend,' said the count, 'and for myself… don't wish it. But in any case, I have an obligation, and I intend to wait patiently until the Lord is pleased to call me to him, once I have paid that debt.'

'What debt? To whom?' asked Voratis.

'When my blood,' replied the old man, '—when my blood ran more quickly, and my arms ran with younger sinews, seeing the vicissitudes of Europe and the continual changes in my fatherland, I dreamt of its complete independence and its establishment as the hearth of freedom for the whole Greek race, and some ill-considered actions, suited to a premature day-dreamer, led the authorities to pursue me; a dangerous matter in those times, as you remember.

'Then someone, to his great danger, helped me to escape, and, as I had gone away, my property was plundered, and, in saving my life, I sacrificed my future. But this person protected my interests, saved my estate, and, as my self-appointed trustee, returned it to me intact and increased.

'Moreover, this same person, at the first suitable opportunity, used his influence to have my name erased from the list of prosecutions.

'See, then, to whom I am in debt; see, then, whom I wish to recompense.'

'You want to compensate *me*?' asked Voratis, in a tone that sounded displeased.

'You don't ask first what sort of compensation I propose, but instead you get angry enough to eat me, you wild man!' said Count Nannetos, smiling.

'I don't ask,' answered Voratis mildly, 'because those acts you have recounted carried with them a hundredfold reward from the happiness I had in doing them. Well, let us see, my dear debtor, what recompense do you propose?'

'Cheap for me,' said the old man, 'but perhaps beneficial for you. A piece of advice.'

'Oh! That, certainly,' exclaimed Voratis happily. 'And I'd accept a hundred, not just one.'

'That wicked young girl there, who seems to be joining her father in fighting against me, and would eat me up with her big eyes, I advise you… to marry her off.'

'Father, if the other ninety-nine pieces of advice are like this first one,' said Angeliki heatedly, 'believe me, you should shut your ears.'

'Oh, the cunning descendant of Odysseus!' said the sick man kindly and merrily. 'She fears the song of the Sirens!'

Voratis bowed his head silently, and a cloud of sadness darkened his brow, but Count Nannetos affected not to notice.

'That is my first piece of advice. My second is that you find her a husband who is worthy of her. I know someone who silently worships her, as one worships the saints, someone who will give her his whole spirit, insofar as it is given to humans here on earth to receive it. Ask her if she would like to hear my third piece of advice, and if she accepts, from my hand Rodini who, lo, with what eloquent silence!, begs through me. But, Rodini my boy, perhaps I misunderstand the reason for your silence?'

Rodini grasped the old man's hand and, kissing it, said:

'My benefactor, you have knocked on the gates of paradise for me, at which I would not dare even to gaze. I await one word for them to open…'

'You hear?' said the count, addressing Angeliki, who was as pale and motionless as an ancient caryatid.

'Beloved friend,' said Voratis, also taking Count Nannetos's hand, 'my daughter is poor. I could never hope more happiness for her than that which I myself could offer with my fatherly affection. But if, honoured friend, you approve her for Rodini; if Rodini accepts her poverty; if her wishes are not against it, then I give her all I have to give: a father's heartfelt good wishes. What do you say, my daughter?'

Angeliki threw herself into his arms, and all her feelings, pent up until then, were released in tears.

'Father,' she said, 'my fate is in your hands. Do with me what you will.'

'My dear Voratis,' added the count, 'don't let it worry you that Rodini isn't rich. He who is both honourable and diligent never fears poverty. God doesn't turn away from his efforts.'

'No treasure,' replied Voratis, 'could be equal to my joy in gaining Rodini as my son; to knowing that my daughter's fate is in hands I trust. Show thanks, my daughter, for the kindness of this father, who grants you such prosperity.'

And so saying, he pushed her gently, until Angeliki was on her knees in front of the old man, and kissed his honoured right hand, thus hiding her face, already blushing like an anemone. At the same time Rodini automatically took the count's left hand; then the count united their hands and placed his own on their heads, raising his eyes to heaven, and seemed for some moments to be praying.

'My friends,' he said then, 'the most fervent of my wishes has been realized here on earth. From now on I shall set my course cheerfully towards death, who knocks on my rotten gate. A father's blessing equips one well for life, and you two have the sincerest of all wishes. If the children's happiness gives pleasure to the souls of dead parents, then be happy, my children, and I too will lie happy in my grave.'

They all threw themselves into his embrace, and tears flowed from their eyes.

'But,' added the good old man, 'I don't know how many drops remain for me at the bottom of life's phial. Perhaps it would seem tiresome for you, my children, if you were asked to hasten the celebration of your union so that I can manage to be present?'

'My dear benefactor,' Voratis answered, 'I hope you live long enough to bless their children as you have blessed them. But I am ready for the marriage to proceed, if you wish, and if dear Rodini is prepared.'

'There is just one duty I must perform first,' said Rodini, 'because it takes precedence for my well-being: I must set out for Corfu, to get my mother's blessing.'

'Go, dearest,' said the count, 'go, and take her a small present from me, and ask for her consent on my behalf. Respect for parents sanctifies life, and the blessings of parents support the household.'

Voratis, with Angeliki and Rodini, got up to take their leave. As Rodini was going, the count called to him:

'Tomorrow before dawn,' he told him, 'my ship, the *Saint Yerasimos*, sets sail for Trieste. Travel with her, don't delay, and be back soon. Be well. When you set out tomorrow, I shall be sleeping.'

Rodini seized his hand again and kissed it, then ran after Angeliki.

Then the old man went to sleep: perhaps the first gentle and sweet sleep in all the days of his long illness, dreaming of the angels smiling on him. And Rodini strode towards his fiancée's house; the angels choosing him, too, to smile upon.

# IV

It was already past midnight when old Nikolos, Count Nannetos's aged servant, who was asleep in the ground floor dining-room, thought, in the confusion of sleep, that he heard muffled footsteps going up the stairs. This roused his drowsy senses.

The footsteps continued upwards, and could be heard louder and heavier on the upper floor. The servant was inclined to jump out of bed, but noticing that the footsteps were going straight to Rodini's room, he remembered that Rodini had gone out with Voratis and his daughter and had not yet come back.

He concluded that it must be him going upstairs, and was even more convinced of this when he heard the footsteps going from Rodini's room towards the count's bedroom, and a conversation going on there. Convinced, as said, that Rodini had come back and, finding the count awake, had talked with him, old Nikolos was reassured and allowed his just-troubled sleep to overcome him again.

From then on the sound of conversation was muffled, and finally he fell into a deep sleep.

At dawn, when the devoted servant awoke, he hastened to his master's bedroom and went in quietly. But since, after he'd waited silently for a few moments, the count didn't speak to him, he left, holding his breath. In the main hall he met Rodini coming out of his room.

'You came back late yesterday, Signor Rodini,' he said to him.

'True, Nikolos old man. But how's the count?'

'Asleep.'

'Asleep? When he wakes up, tell him I wish him good health and say farewell.'

'What? You're going away, Signor Rodini?'

'Yes indeed, my friend, for a few days; it's necessary.'

'And you're not going to wait to say goodbye to the count?'

'I said goodbye to him last night. I can't wait; the boat's leaving.' And so saying he went down and embarked a few minutes later.

At about the same time, an unknown person delivered a sealed letter to the notary and left at once. Tapas opened it and, surprised to find within a sealed document, hid it in his bosom. Then, evidently troubled, he read the letter.

'The bastard!' he exclaimed after reading it. He felt like tearing it up, but changed his mind, opened a secret drawer in his desk, and shut it inside.

'Who knows,' he said, 'what might happen? Who knows?'

An hour after Rodini had left, Nikolos went again, on tiptoe, into the count's bedroom. But as now, too, there was total silence, he left again, so as not to disturb his sleep. He did this three times, at half-hourly intervals. Finally, struck by such a long sleep, he approached the bed, lifted the covers gently, and what was his astonishment when he saw that the pillow was covering the head of the sick man, and what his horror when he saw, removing the pillow, that the old man was dead, and blood had spilt on his face and his sheets!

'The count!' cried the faithful servant, running manically out of the bedroom and tearing his white hair. 'Count Nannetos! Help! Count Nannetos is dead!'

These wild cries roused the neighbours, and the dreadful news went from mouth to mouth in the twinkling of an eye to the whole of Argostoli, in which the aged count was loved and revered as an old patriarch.

The entire distressed population ran to the dead man's house, and various rumours spread among them, which were changed and exaggerated from moment to moment. Some said that apoplexy had caused the count's sudden death, others that robbers had come in the night and killed him, and had taken a large amount of cash from his safe.

Among the first arrivals was Tapas the notary who, because of his profession, had the advantage of usually being informed before others of everything that happened in the town and on the island. Elbowing aside those who had gathered on the stairs, whether going up or down, he went hastily into the room where the dead man lay.

It was apparent that the piteous sight of that respected form, already livid, distorted by agony and all bloody, moved the feelings of Tapas's heart violently, as indeed those of all the bystanders, but his especially, because if all eyes weren't fixed exclusively on the deathbed, it would have been easy for each to see the notary's face turning as pale as the dead man's.

But he quickly conquered the force of his sorrow and, taking into consideration the seriousness of his character, with a respectful hand drew the bed-sheet up to cover the head of the dead man. Then he called in the lamenting Nikolos.

'*Caro*,' he said, 'the poor man was old. An attack of apoplexy has taken him from us. Ai! What boot our tears? Could they wake him? Today this one, tomorrow myself, the next day yourself. Such is man. When he decays, cast him away. Now, *caro*, why did you gather all these people here? We must show a little respect for the dead! The poor fellow has gone to find repose in the other world. We must not make a spectacle of him before the people. Close the door, my boy, and send them out until the priests come. For the good I say it: we must lift him up without noise and with no trouble, just as he lived all his life.'

The faithful servant, readily persuaded by the notary's words, which were in agreement with his own sad inclination, which demanded peace and quiet, asked the assembled people to go away, and the room started to empty, when Voratis rushed in and, out of control, threw himself at the bed and embraced the covered corpse, kissing the shapeless body.

Then Tapas approached the servant and said something to him, and Nikolos went up to Voratis, took him by the arm, and tried with persuasion and gentle force to release him from the object of his despair.

But Voratis remained as one whose mind is convinced, but not his heart.

'Let me see for one last time his venerable face,' he shouted. 'His last words were certainly a wish for me. Let me receive them from his dead lips.'

And, trembling, he lifted the sheet which con-
cealed the count's form. But as soon as he turned it,
he was as one thunderstruck.

'The doctor,' he shouted. 'Run for the doctor!'

'The doctor?' said Tapas. 'What does he want
with the doctor? He has neither life nor breath, the
wretched one. He is dead, *povero amico*.[20] No doctor
can raise him any more.'

'The doctor,' Voratis shouted again, running to
the door. 'At once, bring him at once!'

'Leave it,' said Tapas in a pitying tone of voice.
'Don't you see? Sorrow has clouded your mind.
Come out, *caro* Voratis; come out and let's lock this
room. Be a sensible person: here you will only lose
your mind and your health. Come out, *caro*.'

But at that moment two of the foregathered people who had already gone out with Voratis's first cry,
following his directions, had found a doctor passing
the house, and took him to the bedroom of grief.

Tapas, when he saw him, lowered his glasses in
front of his eyes, as he did automatically when he was
disturbed, or as was his habit when he had to hide
some idea. But was anyone thinking of Tapas?

'Your Excellency,' said Voratis, 'you have heard
that our good old man has died. Approach, Excel-

---

20. 'Poor friend'

lency, and tell us how matters seem to you: what did he die of?'

'Good God, man!' cried Tapas. 'Who could have any doubt? A fearful attack of apoplexy!'

'I have my doubts,' answered Voratis. 'Let the doctor speak.'

Then the doctor approached the dead man. It was clear at a first glance that he was astonished, as Voratis had been, and Tapas too. Then he made a more careful examination, touched the throat with his hand, felt the glands, and, raising his head:

'Signor Nikolos,' he said, 'ask the police to come.'

'Good heavens, what talk is this!' shouted Tapas. 'The police! Won't you let them bury the Christian in peace? You'll make him go to judgement like the Pharaohs of Egypt?'

The servant hesitated, but the doctor was firm.

'I hold you responsible, Signor Nikolos,' he said. 'Inform the police immediately.'

Two minutes later, during which the doctor quietly continued with his investigations, the policeman arrived with the examining magistrate.

'Gentlemen,' the doctor told them, 'Count Nannetos has died. In my opinion, his death was not natural, but violent. Proceed with your responsibilities.'

'Upon what is your opinion based, Excellency?' the policeman asked the doctor.

'The compression of the pharynx,' he replied, gesturing at the items he mentioned, 'the bruising of the neck, the swelling of the glands, exophthalmia, contraction of the facial muscles, twisting of the extremities, and this haemorrhage, a result of the rupture of the jugular vein, unequivocally indicate violent strangulation.'

The doctor's verdict and the fearful exposition of its basis made a deep impression on those present, above all on Voratis, who covered his face with both hands and, unable to overcome the violence of his feelings, felt his strength give way, and fainted as if dead beside his dead friend. Tapas made the necessary arrangements for the patient to be sent home and, with the doctor's approval, he asked that Voratis be put straight to bed.

The pitiable scene had, it seemed, violently moved his heart too, for his lips were lily white.

'By Bacchus,' he said when Voratis came to, 'he who has had such a life as Count Nannetos's must consider matters well. Old and ill, not a related soul to take care of him, here he is at the ends of the earth, alone with old Nikolos. After all, it wouldn't be extraordinary if two rogues came in the night and did him in. That's the sea over there: the murderers will have come from some boat, and now they will have set sail for who knows where. One might look anywhere!'

'It is at least our responsibility, Mr Tapas,' said the policeman, 'to seek until we find.'

Then he asked all on the scene, excluding the examining magistrate, Tapas, the servant, and the doctor, to leave, and addressing the last of them he asked if it were not possible the count had fainted in the night, and the pillows in falling had asphyxiated him. The doctor replied that the facial expression and the disposition of the limbs indicated extreme agony and not sudden death occurring during a faint.

Old Nikolos, directed by the examining magistrate, put the pillows on the dead man's head as he had found them when he first came into the bedroom and it was noticed that it was impossible that his head could have fallen in that way automatically, but that they must have been placed and held there violently.

Then the policeman uncovered the body completely. The sheet was torn near the feet. Asked about this, the servant told him that he had newly spread the sheet on the evening of that day. It was clear then that the victim had torn it in his agony.

Then the policeman started his examination of the furniture. There seemed no trace of anybody having broken into anything. Getting the keys from Nikolos, he opened the desk drawers, and found the sum of up to a thousand *distila* in various gold and silver coins.

Tapas, carrying out the general commission of Count Yerasimos, nephew of the deceased, and furthermore the regular will of the old man, dated a month before his death, confirming Yerasimos as sole heir, demanded that this sum be handed over to him, against a receipt, and the officers of the law did this readily.

After this the policeman examined the windows one by one. All were closed: without breakage, of which there was no sign, it would have been impossible to open them from outside. The doors too were untouched.

'Strange!' said the examining magistrate. 'It seems certain the count was murdered: but burglars don't leave a thousand *distila* in the drawers, nor do they come in through the keyhole. Isn't that true, Signor Tapas?'

'Certainly, certainly!' said the notary, wiping the sweat from his brow.

'And does anyone else live in the neighbourhood of this house?' the examining magistrate asked the servant.

'No one,' he replied, 'except Mr Rodini, the deceased's secretary, and me.'

'And you lock the doors every evening?' added the policeman.

'Indeed, every evening.'

'Do you remember if you closed them yesterday?'

'I remember that I closed them yesterday too, as always.'

'And this morning, when you woke,' the policeman resumed, 'you found them shut?'

'No,' answered Nikolos, 'I found them open. But as Mr Rodini has a spare key, and he returned late last night, I wasn't at all suspicious; I thought he'd forgotten to shut them.'

'Ah! Signor Rodini has a spare key!' said Tapas, and at once his hitherto very pale lips reddened, and in his eyes were lightning flashes, sudden but invisible, because his glasses had misted over.

'Let Mr Rodini come,' said the examining magistrate. 'It's possible he can shed some light on our investigations.'

'Mr Rodini isn't here; he left for Corfu,' said Nikolos.

'What? Yesterday he came home late at night, and this morning he left at cockcrow! *Per Dio Santo!*' said Tapas, speaking to himself, and raising his glasses to his forehead, baring his eyes in an expression of astonishment.

'He's left for Corfu!' interjected the examining magistrate. 'And what time did Rodini return yesterday?'

'Gentlemen,' said Nikolos, frightened, 'You surely don't suspect Rodini of the count's murder!'

'*Caro mio*,' put in the notary, 'Rodini is a golden youth; I love him as I love my eyes. But all men are children of Adam; temptation still has many traps. Besides, amico, in such an important case, justice must investigate, and joy to him who is innocent.'

'Well said,' added the examining magistrate calmly. 'It is our duty to consider all the circumstances. And that is certainly in the interests of the innocent, because it will prove their innocence, so please reply: at what time yesterday did Rodini return?'

'I don't know exactly; midnight, or after midnight,' answered the servant.

'Then for sure,' said Tapas, as if the thought had simply escaped him, 'Signor Nikolos was asleep.'

'Did you see Rodini when he came in?' asked the magistrate.

'No: I heard him. His footsteps woke me, but a little later I fell asleep again.'

'And you didn't hear any other disturbance?'

'I heard Signor Rodini going towards his own bedroom. But instead of going in, he turned and went into the count's. I heard the two of them talking there, and then I fell asleep.'

Tapas threw a meaningful look at the examining magistrate and the policeman.

'And in the morning,' he said, 'when he left, the count was certainly still alive.'

'I don't know, but I don't think so,' Nikolos replied, spilling more tears.

'What? And he had left without bidding him farewell?' the notary asked again. Drawn by his curiosity and his well-established friendship with the deceased he had doubtless forgotten that the right to interrogate didn't belong to him, but the investigating magistrate, knowing his great abilities, conceded this gratefully.

'Without bidding him farewell,' answered Nikolos. 'He told me that he'd said goodbye to him in the evening, because he was in a hurry and didn't want to wake him in the morning.'

The examining magistrate threw a strange look at the policeman, and they both nodded their heads.

'Suspicious, *veramente*,'[21] said Tapas, explaining what was in the minds of the officers of the law. 'But Rodini doesn't cross my mind. What motive had he, what interest in doing it, since he took nothing? Living, the count supported him. Dead, would he inherit?'

And with these latter words, he lowered his glasses.

'In any case,' said the examining magistrate, 'Rodini must come. Then maybe, among other things, the motives will become clear.'

---

21. 'Truly'

Then the police gave permission for burial, which would be carried out with all solemnity. The next day Tapas presented the count's will for legal ratification, and, sending it to Yerasimos, wrote:

'Bad, sad news, Signor Count. Your beloved uncle has kicked the bucket. Accept his will, *povero amico*, and don't you die too from your sorrow. Don't come to Argostoli for a while, where everything will seem black and dark to you. Stay where you are; or seek consolation in travel, until such time as… your sorrow passes.'

# V

So Rodini sailed for Corfu, and since the steam-boat was still rare in those days and the servant of only the richest nations, he went by sailing boat. Great was his impatience, but the weather conditions were indifferent to human impatience. In the end his crossing took four days, which probably seemed to him like four years, as he knew that the return would take at least another four.

It is superfluous to describe his meeting with his mother. In an hour he had expressed his happiness and received his mother's consent and blessing. He showed her the will in which the count left her personally four thousand *distila*, and once he had heard all her eulogies prompted by gratitude to the virtuous count, his eyes were already turning towards the harbour, struggling against her insistent invitation to stay with her for one or two days.

Having as her advocate Rodini's filial affection, she had already won from him several hours, and she per-

suaded him to wait for dinner; at the table she negoti-
ated with him to stay the night, and Rodini came close
to sacrificing some more hours to please her, when the
servant gave him a letter bearing an official seal.

'Who brought it?' Rodini asked.

'Three police constables,' the servant replied, 'and
they're waiting in the courtyard.'

Rodini opened the letter, and was obviously disturbed.

'See, Mother,' he said, smiling, but in a changed
voice, 'I have an ally against you.'

'What ally?'

'The Cephalonian police. They want me to return
without delay.'

'What? When you've only just arrived? On whose
orders? And what if you don't want to go tonight, but
wait until tomorrow...'

'The bailiffs are under orders to take me against
my will.'

'But what's this? Oh, my God! What's going on?'
exclaimed the devoted mother. 'The police are *arrest-
ing* you... what's this?'

'On what order, I don't know myself,' answered
Rodini, 'but calm down, Mother; it can't be anything
serious. Let's call the bailiffs.'

One of the bailiffs, who had been sent from
Cephalonia as the bearer and executor of orders,

approached Rodini with a hesitant step, while the other two, given to him as assistants by the police station in Corfu, stood as if guarding the way out.

'Well, Signor Janeto,' asked Rodini, 'They have requested that I return to Cephalonia? Do you know, or are you allowed to tell me, what it's about?'

The bailiff seemed troubled.

'Sir,' he said, 'Count Nannetos has died and... there is a suspicion he was murdered. The police are investigating, and they're asking for you as... a witness.'

This explanation made different impressions on mother and son: she entertained fears, while he seemed thunderstruck.

'The count...! Dead...! Murdered...! Oh my God!' he shouted, becoming as pale as the wall, and falling, overcome by grief, into the arms of his mother. The bailiffs exchanged meaningful glances.

Then Rodini said farewell to his mother.

'Let's go, gentlemen,' he said to the bailiffs. 'Happiness and longing can wait, but the duties of mourning cannot.'

In a little while they set off in the police craft, and after some days they sailed into Argostoli.

When Rodini disembarked he wanted to go to the grave of his benefactor and offer the libation of his tears, but the bailiffs told him that they had orders to take him directly to the police.

Following these instructions, he was presented to the police, and asked permission to go, but the policeman told him he had orders to hold him, and he handed him over to the cell custodian, who told him he had orders not to let him communicate with anybody, and put him in solitary confinement.

Rodini thought he must be dreaming, and was unable to understand what was going on: sometimes he suspected that the government, while investigating a plot (a product of the overwhelming enthusiasm of the Greeks of the Ionian Islands at the time of the beginnings of the Greek revolution), had arrested him following an unsubstantiated lead; sometimes that he was simply arrested in the place of someone else as a result of a police error. All night he jumped from one conclusion to another, but his own concerns were drowned in his sorrow over the death of his benefactor, his second father.

The next day, in the morning, he was committed to the court, to his great joy, because the interrogation would make his situation clear. Behold, then, the formal interrogatory dialogue:

'What is your name?'

'Athanasios Rodini.'

'What is your country?'

'Corfu.'

'What is your age?'

'Twenty-four.'

'What is your profession?'

'Secretary to Count Nannetos.'

'Where did you learn of the death of Count Nannetos?'

'In Corfu, from the policemen who brought me here.'

'At what time?'

'On Thursday morning.'

'How did you leave Count Nannetos when you set out?'

'Asleep.'

'How did you know he was asleep?'

'His servant told me.'

'And you didn't go in to say goodbye?'

'No, I didn't want to disturb his sleep.'

'It seems strange that, although it's known that you were so intimate with the count, you shouldn't want to say goodbye before your departure.'

'I had said goodbye to him in the evening, knowing that I would set out very early.'

'In the evening you went out of the house. Where did you go, and what time did you come back?'

'I left and went to Tapas the notary, then to Mr Voratis, with whom I went to see the count. Then I went back with Mr Voratis to his house, where I stayed until one in the morning, and then I went back home.'

'On your return to the house, where did you go and what did you do?'

'I went to my room, packed for the journey, and went to bed.'

'When you returned to the house, was the outer door closed?'

'I found it open, and thought the servant had left it so for me.'

'Do you have a key for that door?'

'I have.'

Then the judge called Tapas, who stated that after midday on the ninth of the month Rodini did indeed come to his office, that in the presence of various of his clients asked him to advance him a loan of a thousand *distila*, saying that soon he would have the means to pay it back, and when insistently asked about this he said, in particular, that Count Nannetos had left him all his wealth in a privately drawn up will.

Tapas added that he didn't want to proceed further with organizing the loan, suspecting some irregularity, because he knew that one month earlier Count Nannetos had bequeathed his fortune, by a notarised will, to his nephew, and if since then he had wanted to change all or part of it, he would have, in the normal course of affairs and according to an article in his will, made a proper codicil in that document.

This deposition seemed of little interest to the investigating magistrate.

After Tapas, those clients present at his office on the ninth were called, and all agreed they had heard Rodini asking for the loan and saying that he would have sufficient land to secure tenfold the thousand *distila*.

Voratis, called after them, confirmed that in the early evening of the ninth Rodini had come to his house and accompanied him and his daughter to the count's, and on being questioned related how, at the instigation of the count, Angeliki and Rodini became engaged.

'Forgive me if I seem to be interfering in your home relations,' said the judge mildly. 'Do understand that I confine myself exclusively to only what may light me towards discovering the truth. Rodini is poor. Count Nannetos didn't tell you that when he proposed him to you as your son-in-law?'

'The count told me that although Rodini had no riches, he had the possibility to become rich because of his honourability.'

'On the evening of his death then,' continued the judge, 'the count didn't tell you he had made Rodini his heir?'

'Rodini his heir!' exclaimed Voratis. 'No! He didn't say that. That is a libel against Rodini.'

'And you left the count's with Rodini that evening?' the judge asked again.

'Indeed.'

'And at what time did Rodini leave your house?'

'At one o'clock, after midnight.'

Then Nikolos was questioned, answering exactly as he had answered at his first questioning, insisting that when Rodini returned to the house that night he had gone to the count's bedroom, and that he had heard from there conversation with the old man. Asked if he knew that the count had made Rodini his heir, he replied that he had never heard anything about it.

Then the judge called Rodini back again.

'On the ninth of the month,' he said, 'you requested the notary to arrange a loan of a thousand *distila* for you. Can you explain to us what need you had of this sum?'

And, seeing that Rodini hesitated to answer, he added: 'Remember that you are obliged to tell us the whole truth.'

'If the court,' said Rodini, 'needs, for its enlightenment, to penetrate into the depths of my private life, then although I regret it, I am willing to reveal it. I did in fact ask for the loan, but only provisionally. It is a matter of my asking for the hand of Angeliki Voratis. Only if my proposal were accepted would I have had need of the loan.'

'But you told the notary you were able to provide security to the creditors in the form of land ten times its value. You don't have land in Cephalonia. What was your idea?'

'Indeed I don't have land,' he replied, 'but Count Nannetos had left me his. You see then why I asked for the loan: because while he still lived that could not be realized; I didn't wish to touch his property.'

'Count Nannetos made you his heir? But doesn't he have a nephew? How, then?'

'It is not for me,' said Rodini, avoiding answering the enigma in the question, 'to judge the reasons why the count left his fortune to another, rather than to his nephew.'

'And he left a will appointing you as his heir?'

'Yes, indeed.'

Rodini took the will from his bosom and handed it to the prosecutor, who read it very attentively.

'The signature is the count's?' he asked finally.

'Yes, indeed,' answered Rodini calmly.

'But its writing doesn't resemble that of the document itself.'

'No, certainly it doesn't,' he answered, 'because the document was not in his own hand.'

'Ah! Then in whose hand?' the magistrate asked suspiciously.

'In my own.'

'In your own? How come?'

'Yes,' Rodini answered simply. 'He dictated to me, and I wrote.'

'Ah! He dictated, Mr Rodini, and you wrote,' said the judge, casting him a sharp glance. 'And when did he dictate and you write the will, may I ask?'

'On the ninth of the month, around the middle of the day.'

'Ah! The ninth?' the judge remarked ironically. 'The last day of his life. How fortunate, Mr Rodini, that he didn't wait until the tenth.'

Rodini brought his handkerchief to his eyes.

'This tragic display can wait until the final day of the trial,' said the judge bitterly. 'Then it might have some significance. For the moment, return to prison.'

While Rodini had hoped that his interrogation would enlighten both himself and the judge, and that the gates of the prison would open at once, he was thrown in again, with the fearful conviction that he was considered a suspect in the murder of the count.

# VI

From then on orders were given that he should be
guarded more strictly, and no one was allowed to
visit him. The gathering of evidence, the examination
of witnesses, some of whom, such as Rodini's mother,
were in Corfu, took over a month. Finally came the
day of the trial, and an innumerable crowd, such as
never before at any judicial proceedings, flooded the
court. The audience had gathered not just from all
parts of Cephalonia but also from the adjacent
islands, even from Corfu, because the abhorrent
murder of such a respected man as Count Nannetos,
philanthropic, and generally loved for his fine character, gave rise to general consternation; and though
a few, who had confidence in the goodness and
virtue of Rodini, couldn't believe in his guilt, in most
the crime inspired horror, because such revolting
ingratitude had never been heard of, and never had
a parricide been perpetrated under more abhorrent
circumstances.

When the accused was brought forth, his silent gaze and his courageous step showed his clear conscience only to those who knew him; to the rest they seemed symptoms of unfeeling disrespect, hardened wickedness, and the feelings of the listeners for or against him was stretched to the limit.

To begin with, the previous witnesses were examined anew, and the depositions of the absentees were read.

Among the first of the witnesses, old Nikolos excited general attention and sympathy. He was dressed from head to foot in black, with grey hair like his master's and with his head bowed to the ground, as if burdened with twice his years since that day, and his sorrow was written on his brow and in the redness of his eyes. The indubitable honesty of his words, and the fact that he explained the events of that night differently from Rodini, made the greatest impression on both the audience and the judges.

Voratis's sorrow was no less. When he appeared before the court and saw Rodini in the dock, he wanted to throw himself into his arms, but the ushers prevented him. Once he'd recovered, he repeated his evidence, and especially emphasised that the old man had made no will in favour of Rodini, convinced that this was the truth, and that the truth is always the ally of the innocent.

Rodini wanted to speak, but the chief judge ordered him to be silent until asked.

When Tapas came to give evidence he had his spectacles on: a smile on his face insinuated sympathy towards the accused and a modesty about himself; he tried to lend charm to his voice and, speaking in honeyed tones, said that the accused was for him, always 'the honourable Signor Rodini,' 'the estimable Signor Rodini,' and sometimes '*carissimo Signor* Rodini.' So he stated that 'the estimable Signor Rodini,' some hours before malefactors murdered poor Count Nannetos, had told him that he was sure to have great riches in a little while; that he assured him of the existence of a will by the count which made him his sole legatee and that this seemed strange to Tapas himself, because a month earlier the count had registered a will in his office and any change to it would have to be added in the form of a codicil. Asked about the signature on the privately made will, Tapas said it resembled the count's, but there seemed to him some difference.

When the examination of the witnesses had been completed, the public prosecutor took the floor. And he spoke in Italian, as speaking Greek in the court was still not allowed in the Ionian Islands. Indeed at the time, an inhabitant of the islands presenting himself in front of the court would listen to the public prosecutor and his defence lawyer talk, while his honour, his property and even his life were in jeopardy, and he wouldn't understand a word.

So the public prosecutor spoke in Italian, but he did talk with great eloquence and vehemence. His reasoning was tight and seemed incontrovertible. He mentioned all the circumstances, the grounds showing unequivocally that the count had been murdered. He reminded the court that the house door had been found open and in no way forced on the morning after the crime, so that it must without doubt have been opened with a key, and that apart from the faithful servant Nikolos, who stood to gain nothing by the death of his master and whom he worshipped, who else had a key to the house except Rodini? He explained that the murderer was not a burglar, because the count's money and possessions had been found untouched. Who then could have an interest in committing this horrific crime, who was to gain by it, if not Rodini, who presented himself, in order to reap the fruit, with the count's will in hand?

But this will, by which, from the depths of penury, Rodini would gain great riches, whose was it? Entirely written in *his* hand, and bearing only the alleged signature of the count, and that brought into question by the most credible witnesses. And as such, private and unofficial, this will, cancelling a preexisting and notarised one, without being a codicil, clearly contradicted the first. And when was it drawn up? A few hours before the crime. And when did Rodini present it? Once the crime had been committed, once the count was no longer there to show it a lie. So who could doubt it? Either the will was forged or it was signed by force.

Then Rodini returns to the house after midnight on the night of the crime, enters the count's bedroom, and talks with him. Why should he deny it? The count was still living then: in the morning he is found the victim of murderers' hands. Why does Rodini, as soon as dawn comes, escape from the island in a great hurry? Why does he leave without even going into the old man's bedroom, when the servant urged him to do so? The public prosecutor concluded by saying that Rodini faked the will and murdered the count; that he didn't suggest the penalty to be imposed but left it to the appraisal of the judges, because he knew the cruelty of lions, the bloodthirstiness of tigers, but such a degree of bestiality he didn't know from even the wildest beasts, nor did he know of any nation whose penal code was appropriate to the enormity of such vileness.

Rodini listened to this profusion of reasoning with growing astonishment. The reasoning of the servant of justice seemed so correct, and his inferences so valid, that he felt that he himself would be convinced, had he not the consciousness of his own innocence.

Finally he got up slowly and with dignity, when the prosecutor had finished, and said that his sorrow unto death was the pitiful end of his honoured benefactor for whom he had a son's love; that the fullest measure of his unhappiness, the suspicion that he himself had murdered his second father, he had already accepted without so much as a murmur, since he could see the strange chain of coincidences which

suggested his guilt; that he didn't request a lawyer, putting his hope in the power of simple truth. And if this seemed so difficult to unravel, he would not take refuge in technicalities; that in opposition to the appearances he could offer nothing more than his simple denial.

He repeated that Count Nannetos had voluntarily dictated and then signed the will, but insistently refused to say whether he knew what reasons had persuaded the count to do this; he added that the count had never said a word to him about a previous will, that on that evening he had given him permission to leave for Corfu in the morning, that they had made their farewells then so that he shouldn't come into his bedroom in the morning and disturb his sleep, and that he had left knowing nothing of the fearful crime. He said that this was all his defence, and if appearances were against him, the truth took precedence. Having said that, he calmly sat down.

The feebleness of this defence seemed to everyone to augur badly; those who had been undecided shook their heads threateningly, while Rodini's friends hid their faces, and Voratis started to weep like a child, foreseeing no good conclusion.

The court retired to consider; the audience was violently agitated, and there were muffled murmurs like a troubled sea when a storm is about to break. So when the judges returned an hour later to pronounce the death penalty for forgery and murder, not one word of pity for the condemned was heard, but indeed there were cheers for the clear justice of the decision.

Not one word of pity, as I said, because for the rest of the audience, horror towards a cruel criminal was stronger than pity towards an acquaintance, while Voratis, when he heard the fearful sentence, fainted, and was taken out of the courtroom.

But again there was deceitfulness, because that compassionate notary Tapas, coming away from the public gallery, was heard to say several times, 'The miserable bastard!' 'Poor guy!'

When Voratis recovered, he hurried to the prison, where he found his friend neither faint-hearted, nor indifferent to or disdainful of life; rather, greatly surprised at what life had brought him and almost unable to put his thoughts together.

'A pardon, make haste to ask for pardon,' cried Voratis. 'The law gives you a time limit of six weeks. Hurry and ask for pardon.'

'Pardon!' Rodini replied, opening his eyes as if dazzled. 'If I am still permitted to ask for *justice* I do so readily; but the guilty ask for pardon, and I'm not guilty. I shan't ask for it.'

'But they will execute you, and there's no other recourse.'

'They will execute me,' said Rodini, turning pale. 'I heard, and I regret from the depths of my heart that I am executed in disastrously misunderstood circumstances, the judges' unhappy delusion. I am sorry to abandon life so young, and just at the moment when life was about to offer me the horn of Amalthi, containing all happiness. For a moment my union with Angeliki was revealed to me like the sight of God, my life's secret worship; the breath of early death will extinguish that sight, as well as the enjoyment of riches I was about to experience because Count Dionysios Nannetos—whose death would have been the only cloud in the rest of my life— Count Dionysios had made me his heir.

'What? My dear Rodini, you're saying…'

'You see,' answered Rodini with a bitter smile, 'my condemnation gave the right to even my closest friends to doubt my word. Yes, I tell you that Count Nannetos left me his entire inheritance in his will and you hear it for the first time from my mouth because the will was in fact written on the last day before the count's death, and in addition because the count didn't wish you to know it as long as he still lived.'

Voratis clapped his hands to his head.

'Ill fortune! Ill fortune!' he cried. 'You must admit, my friend, that one needs to have limitless faith in you, as I do, in order to believe this.'

'I admit it,' Rodini replied, 'and for that I'm not impatient with my judges, I don't have the right to expect from them a similar faith.'

'But the other will, made out to his nephew...!'

'About that, I tell you again what I said at the trial, that the count said not a word. Its existence seems to me an incxplicable mystery. The late Count Dionysios, in dictating this will to me, couldn't have mentioned that one, and indeed didn't; on the contrary, when I intervened on behalf of his nephew, he gave me a lengthy explanation, and told me that his final emphatic wish was that not the smallest share of his property should go to his nephew Yerasimos. The circumstance seemed mysterious to me, and I was obliged to seek the solution to this unfairness while I lived.'

'But you must, must live,' Voratis answered, embracing him. 'Ask for pardon, that you may live.'

'That I want to live,' answered Rodini vehemently, 'that I have a reason to live, you know. But you want me to fetter myself, and all my life drag the weight of dishonour? To offer Angeliki a name she would blush to own? You want people to point at me as a new Cain, notorious for his inhumanity, whom the government pardoned but whom God will never forgive? The judges found me guilty by mistake. They have the power; let them execute me. But I'm not guilty, and I shall never buy my life with such a shameful confession. I shall not ask for pardon.'

Voratis took Rodini's hand and squeezed it in his own, shedding a torrent of tears.

'So be it. You don't ask for pardon, since you are asking for justice. If you have the slightest love for me, the slightest compassion for… Angeliki, look to your salvation. Allow me to petition for you, and I will leave no door uncalled at, no stone unturned, and if proper justice still exists on earth, you shall be saved.'

Rodini, unabashed to the end, wrote his petition, but in a manner very different from the usual petitions for pardon. He said that, since he was innocent of the crime for which he was condemned, he asked for the annulment of his condemnation. Voratis took the document and went to present it, hoping to add by his words what was missing from it.

# VII

Having followed Rodini up to now, I must talk again of the most charming character in my drama, Angeliki. Her heart, having painfully taken in Rodini's conduct when he didn't even feel like noticing her beloved Bengal rose on the staircase of the house, was radiant with happiness, like the rose in the spring zephyr, when the count gave her hand to Rodini.

With blushing cheeks and a smile on her lips she walked beside her fiancé when they returned to her father's house following that event, or stood beside him on the balcony after they'd returned and listened to his passionate words. More than half the night passed in murmurings of mutual pledges, hopes, promises and plans for long-lived happiness, in defiance of their circumstances, because their happiness was the fruit of their love, which was beyond external factors, and no future circumstances could separate them; not even death could divide the insoluble bond of their souls.

And when it was past midnight, and Rodini, who in the manner of lovers had repeated a thousand times the same things in different words, eventually left, Angeliki's heart and imagination, both wide awake until dawn, energetically turned the future's bright kaleidoscope, whose flowers, as they poured into her mind, wove themselves into choice bridal crowns, and among the pleasant pictures that made her smile, her all-gold bridal gown was not the least; and its fine fabric stayed in her mind for some time as she considered the design, sketching out the details.

By dawn, when she woke, or rather when she got up, because not having slept she didn't wake, the choice of material had been made. But that day the funeral bell for Count Dionysios was heard from Argostoli, and Angeliki put on mourning rather than bridal clothes.

But since for three whole days she had been deep in tears for the death of her father's and her fiancé's honoured friend, on this fourth day, as a distraction from her sadness, she started to embroider the choice material, pleased that, in the absence of Rodini, she was busy with work that related to him.

As far as he could, Voratis kept the transporting and imprisonment of Rodini from his daughter, finding various excuses for his extended absence. Finally, unable to hide the truth from her completely, he told her that Rodini had arrived from Cephalonia, but that because thorough investigations were being made into the count's murder, the court, hoping that he above all, as one who had lived with the old man and was his friend, could shed light on the matter, had ordered that he should not communicate with anybody until investigations had been completed, and that was why it was not possible for Rodini to come and see them.

Her father's very first words made Angeliki jump; then she was deathly still until she'd heard the last, hearing which she started to cry helplessly. But, feeling that her tears were childish, she calmed down, and resolved to wait patiently until investigations were completed, and completion of the investigation was as far as she was concerned the day of the trial, as her father, certain that Rodini would be absolved, had told her.

Angeliki counted the days, the hours, and the minutes in anxious uneasiness, and when she learnt that the final day had come, her gaze was glued to the sun, measuring its course, and with unhappiness noted its slowness.

At last, towards evening, she heard a sound on the stairs, towards which she all but threw herself. But instead of seeing, as she'd hoped, Rodini flying joyfully up them, she suddenly encountered her father, pale and immobile, being carried up by four men. Her blood ran to her heart. She took the water jar to dampen his forehead, but her hands shook so much she had to put it down, and she was in danger of falling lifeless upon him; she felt that her father's fainting was a harbinger of evil. When he recovered, having received the appropriate treatment:

'Father!' she exclaimed, throwing herself into his embrace, deeply distressed and in floods of tears, 'Father, something dreadful must have happened!'

Voratis, having decided to set out to take care of saving his friend, felt that it was impossible for the frightful tidings not to reach his daughter, and that it was better she should take the bitter cup from his hands rather than those of a stranger.

'My daughter,' he replied, 'life is a continuous struggle, and only the strong-hearted can bear it. We didn't choose it, my daughter: it was given to us, with all its enjoyments and all its calamities, and we must accept it as it was given, and any complaint is a lack of respect. Thus, my dearest Angeliki, many apparent misfortunes are only sent to us as trials of our faith and perseverance, and if we undergo these bravely, eventually they often result at last in joy and reward. Not every cloud, my daughter, brings a thunderbolt: often it brings an invigorating rain. And now what a fearful appearance of unhappiness hangs over us...'

'What, Father, what? Tell me.'

'But it's only an appearance. I went out at once this evening, and I am confident, I have the strong conviction that Rodini will be saved, that it is a simple matter of a mistake by the judges… he was found guilty.'

'Guilty! Guilty! Oh my God, guilty! And who found him guilty?'

'How does it concern us how and what they talked about? Is our fate to be brought down by their hands?' added Voratis, passing the limits of truth a little in reassuring her. 'I am going to meet their superiors, those who hold our lives and deaths in their hands. They will deliver justice to the innocent, and will save him.'

'Father! They have condemned Rodini to death!' Angeliki exclaimed, and her eyes flashed fire; she clutched her temples between her hands, and at that moment her face lost all colour: she looked like a statue of horror or madness.

'They will be ashamed when, in a few days, he returns: I will take him triumphantly out of his prison.'

'They've got him in prison then!' Angeliki exclaimed, her feelings recalling her father's last words. 'Father, take me to his prison. When, an innocent victim, he is led to his death, his fiancée's place is beside him.'

'But, thoughtless child, I told you that I shall save him. He is innocent, and we don't live in an era when it's possible for the innocent to be unjustifiably condemned.' (At this point he again exaggerated somewhat, in an effort to console his daughter.) 'Don't worry. When I come back, I promise you we'll go to his prison together, and it will be you yourself who releases his bonds.'

'You promise me, Father, you promise me! When you come back, I'll go with you to his prison? "For good or ill", you promise me?'

'"For good or ill", I promise you, but calm down.'

'Come then; don't delay even a moment, and may God guide your steps. But when will you return, Father?'

'Sooner or later, I don't know, but in no circumstances is it possible to delay beyond six weeks,' said Voratis, melancholically bowing his head towards the ground.

'Six weeks! Oh my God!' exclaimed his daughter. 'And can a person live six weeks with such anxiety? So be it; I shall try.'

But Angeliki lived those six weeks; she lived every minute of the six weeks, because each one was as full of emotion as a whole year of normal life. All her life's energy was internal, only very little was visible externally. Without putting aside her dark clothes, which she'd put on for the death of Count Dionysios, Angeliki carried on embroidering her bridal clothes, but in many places stains marked the embroidery; tear stains, because ever since the well-springs of her tears had opened, they hadn't closed.

Finally, around dawn on the last day of the six weeks, her gaze turned ceaselessly to the furthest points of the sea-horizon, she discovered a white mark at its edge, and the strong beating of her heart told her that this was the boat that brought the fate of Rodini. As the day wore on the mark got bigger, and as the sun westered a big ship anchored in Argostoli harbour, and Voratis disembarked.

Angeliki waited for him at the courtyard gate of the house and when she saw him she threw herself into his embrace. 'Father,' she exclaimed, 'Father, he is saved! Let's go! Let's go and release his bonds.'

But then she felt her hands wet with tears falling from her father's eyes. Then she heard a wailing, like a child's, from his breast, and then, looking, she noticed for the first time that his forehead was lined with the wrinkles of age, that his hair had turned white, that, in those six weeks, forty winters had fallen on him.

'Ah! I understand,' she said. 'They will kill him! Oh, horror! Oh, horror!'

And with that word her speech expired, her head leant on her father's breast like a lily broken by the storm, and her eyes closed.

The outcome of the court's considerations was that there were no mitigating circumstances; indeed, it spoke severely of the double crime, burdened by black ingratitude. Thus, for all the efforts of Voratis, no reason was found for mercy, even more so since the petition for pardon had been feeble, indeed it seemed only the impudent provocation of a hardened criminal.

'Courage,' said Voratis, embracing her, giving her needed comfort. 'Courage, my daughter. Let us bear this misery, and God will send us, will give us, if not in this world, then in the next, his crown.'

'Yes, courage!' said Angeliki, opening her eyes. 'Behold, I am courageous, oh Father. Come, let us go to the prison.'

'To the prison? What are you saying? Angeliki! Don't seek such a terrible meeting! Even a man's heart could not bear it.'

'You told me "For good or ill", Father, that you would take me to Rodini's prison. Behold, now is the day of ill, on which bad fortune comes down like a black harpy; on which the earth has become a dark abyss, on which the heavens are a pall. Let us not waste time, Father. His prison is now the only place on earth where the sun shines. Let us go to his prison.'

'My Angeliki, that sight is not one for you; the prison is no place for you. Seek consolation, my unhappy daughter, in religion.'

'Father,' said Angeliki, 'may God forgive me if I blaspheme, but I feel that there exist extreme sorrows against which even religion is powerless. My place in future is wherever my fiancé is: if in prison, then in prison; and in his grave, when he is laid in his grave. There exists yet a sight for my eyes, the spectacle of his death, after which all other sights are closed to me.'

'My Angeliki, my Angeliki,' exclaimed Voratis, hugging her to his breast, 'don't kill me. Give me your promise that you will endure this, and remain a brave daughter.'

'Let us not waste these precious moments,' said Angeliki firmly. 'Take me to the prison, lest I die here from hopelessness, or go mad, cursing the day I was born, and I promise; I promise whatever you want.'

Voratis felt that the risk would be more serious if he went against Angeliki's wish than if he acceded to it, and with a breaking heart he conducted her to the prison, arriving when night had already fallen, and asked permission to see the condemned man.

Rodini, not yet knowing his fate or the outcome of his petition, when he saw the door open and Voratis and his daughter coming in, got up from his straw bed and ran towards them, taking their hands:

'You came after all,' he exclaimed. 'You came, I see you again! Oh, my friends, thank you. Behold, the happiest moment of my life. Oh, what long dark hours I have lived apart from you, longer than the aeons of death! How monotonously the days came and how mournfully they passed! The only thing that could attract my attention was golden Venus, when she appeared on my narrow horizon, because my impassioned heart persuaded me, my dear Angeliki, that I saw in her rays every evening your smiling look. And now I had my eyes fixed on her, and my mind flew to you on the wings of freedom, when, friends, you came in bringing me that heavenly gift. From your mouths I accept it, doubly beloved. You, Father, bought it for me with your struggles; you, my dear Angeliki, come to me like an angel of freedom.'

With these words Angeliki hid her face in her hands, and started to weep bitterly, while Voratis took Rodini's hand:

'Freedom, my friend,' he told him, 'freedom does not have its habitation in the filth of this world, in which injustice wallows, where wickedness grazes, where innocence suffers and is persecuted. Freedom dwells in heaven. Fortunate is he who, before passing through this miserable vale of sadness, before drain-

ing all the terrible cup of life to the dregs, is able to
fly to a more perfect world, which is free. Fortunate
is he among us who is first invited to his bosom by
the all-good God, and unhappy are those who are
forgotten behind him!'

And he said this with a trembling voice and full
of tears, so that Rodini, looking in great surprise
at first Voratis and then at his daughter, could not
understand the meaning of these melancholy words
and these extreme signs of sadness, coming as they
did from the messengers of joy.

But before he could resolve his doubt, at that moment the turnkey came in, accompanied by a priest.

'Sir,' he said to Rodini, 'I bring your Most Rev-
erend person. Perhaps in these moments you have
need of his help, because to me has fallen the sad
duty of announcing that the decision of the court…
has been confirmed.'

'Confirmed,' said Rodini calmly. 'I understand.
Thank you, sir, for your philanthropic care. Soon
I shall take refuge in the spiritual help of the Holy
Father. Fetch me ink, please, pen and paper.'

The turnkey left, and Rodini, taking the hand of
the young girl, said:

'Angeliki, you heard what your father said. Fortunate is he who abandons this corrupt world and
goes to a better. Don't cry, my friend. Blessed is he

who can come into the presence of his Maker and bring him a pure soul, a heart without sin. Don't cry. Our premature separation breaks my heart, but what is this separation? It is a mere moment in comparison with eternity, where we shall be united in heaven. I shall wait for you there, and with the rays of sunset my soul shall come down to your forehead as you sleep, and will talk of me to you in your dreams.'

'From the moment that Count Dionysius joined our hands,' Angeliki replied formally, 'I promised you that neither life nor death would be able to separate us for the rest of our lives. Behold, the fearful time of trial has come. No, you will not wait for me. Together we shall go to condemnation, and if the people, adding heartlessness to injustice, will not kill me with you, I shall find a way to come with you, and our souls will rise together to their eternal home.'

'Flowers are scattered over the dead', said Rodini, taking and kissing her hand with passion. 'You, my friend, scatter on my grave the greatest consolation. These words fill the measure of my happiness on earth. After that, life owes me nothing further.'

'Friend,' said the girl, 'did you know what I was doing from the time you were gone? All day I embroidered my wedding dress, and every evening I watered the Bengal rose. Tomorrow, Father, she added with a bitter smile, will be my wedding day. Please do not deny me this joy: to dress me in my wedding dress and to make my bridal crown with the Bengal rose.'

Voratis could bear this scene no longer; his heart was in danger of breaking. He threw himself into the arms of his daughter, weeping like a baby.

'My Angeliki, my daughter,' he said, weeping bitterly, 'how you tear at your father's breast! Come, my daughter, come; let us leave. The time is over, and the prison will close.'

'Leave?' said Angeliki. 'And where would we go, Father? Is there another place on earth for me? This is my home, Father; leave me in it. Yes, I shall in reality depart tomorrow for another home, and that will be eternal.'

'Oh my God, my God! Her mind has given way, Rodini,' exclaimed the unhappy father, as if asking for his help.

'Angeliki,' said Rodini, seeing the heat of her feelings, and how dangerous it would be for her to stay. 'My dear Angeliki, I thought you would take your leave of me with a smile on your lips and hope in your heart. Shall the tie between our souls be less strong, because mortal bodies shall now come between them? And was our love so ephemeral in its nature that it can be conquered by a miscarriage of justice, and what if, instead of this, came a bullet, or an attack of fever? Be patient, sister, and endure. Don't destroy your life with a crime: the punishment might be deprivation of our eternal union and our endless happiness, to which we look forward with confidence.'

'I have no need to cut the thread of my life with violence,' Angeliki whispered. 'It will break by itself. Behold, the beating of my heart will shatter my breast by tomorrow, and I feel I shall precede you to our heavenly home.'

'Go and rest, friend,' said Rodini. 'You need rest. And accept my first, and, on this earth, my last, kiss.'

And he gave her a brotherly kiss on the lips.

'To rest?' she said, smiling mournfully. 'There is no hurry: tomorrow I can rest. Don't ask me to leave. Don't ask that we be apart at all in these last moments.'

'But you must leave,' her father insisted, because he wanted to take her away from such terrible impressions as might soon kill her. 'Rodini needs to be alone.'

'Indeed, friend of my heart,' said Rodini, 'I need to be alone for some hours; alone with the minister of God, and then alone with God Himself.'

'Come, my daughter,' said Voratis, drawing Angeliki towards the door.

'So we are separated!' cried Angeliki in a heart-breaking voice. 'Behold, our last separation. Tomorrow morning, I promise you, I shall be near you, and from then on we shall nevermore be parted.'

Then Voratis fell into the arms of Rodini, and wanted to speak, but tears choked his voice.

'My mother, my poor mother!' said Rodini. 'May she not learn the manner of her son's death. Let her believe that illness took me. Comfort her if you can. She had such love for me! And now, go. My final wishes I will tell you tomorrow.'

Voratis went out, drawing with him his almost senseless daughter. But Angeliki didn't want to go home, and, finding the door of the neighbouring church of Agios Dionysius open, she went in and fell on her knees in front of the sanctuary, and stayed there praying until dawn.

Once Rodini was alone, he took the pen and wrote his will, making Voratis his heir, saying that Count Nannetos's will was genuine, and asking his heir imperatively to seek proof of its genuineness and demand from the court its validation.

After that he came before the priest and very humbly confessed that there were many sins in his life, but he was innocent of the crime for which he had been condemned, even though the priest urged him many times, in the name of the Saviour of his soul, to confess his guilt, and to ask forgiveness and mercy, but none of this advice caused him to alter his confession. Afterwards he requested Holy Communion, and when the priest left he remained deep in prayer until dawn, and certainly his wishes frequently coincided with those of Angeliki, as they rose to the throne of the Creator.

# VIII

In the evening of the day on which this story began, we saw how downcast Marina, the notary's tender daughter, became because Count Yerasimos had left suddenly, without even saying goodnight to her, without even trying her cherries. Her father's words had temporarily cajoled her out of this mood, but she spent all that night in anticipation of the next day, and all the next day in anticipation of the evening (when Yerasimos would return) making up judicious remarks which would show him, in a charming way, her anger at his behaviour, no matter what her father said.

But the evening came, and Yerasimos didn't. Tapas, from her ceaseless comings and goings, her gazing through the window and her going down to the door, saw her anxiety. So when dinner time came and they sat at the table, he said:

'It seems, my daughter, that we shall eat your cherries ourselves. You wait for Count Yerasimos in vain; he won't come.'

'I'm not waiting for Yerasimos,' said Marina, shaking her head in a manner that expressed a sulky reticence.

'You're not waiting for him? Ah! *Veramente*? And I thought you were, when I saw how you made me wait two hours for the meal, and you laid a third place, and next to it the biggest cherries from your garden. So you're not waiting for him? So much the better, because you shouldn't expect him for some days.'

'What! Some days?' exclaimed Marina with a screech, showing that, on the contrary, she had been expecting him, and was uneasy and very much enraged that she didn't see him coming.

'Count Yerasimos,' Tapas replied, 'had, my daughter, pressing work, very pressing, and had to leave. He couldn't waste even uno minuto. For a little while he won't be able to leave it without compromising his interests.'

'For a little while? For how long?' asked Marina.

'How long? How long? How should *I* know? Ten days, fifteen days,' said the notary, not wanting to sadden her.

'What? Fifteen days?' Marina exclaimed despairingly.

'His interests are your interests, *cara mia*,' said her father. 'When he returns, he will be yours. Then you will become the richest, proudest and most praised contessa in Cephalonia and the Ionian Islands. Today you heard that the old count had died. *Povero* Yerasimos isn't here to close his eyes, but he is about to get an inheritance second to none. A little patience, *carissima*. Until he comes, take *consolazione* [22] in his letters.'

'Yes,' said Marina in a sad voice, 'if his great affairs let him write to us.'

She promised, however, to be patient as her father had asked. But she promised before she had estimated her endurance, because her impatience began the very next day. Tapas, in whose heart, as we have said, fatherly love was the only human feeling that had survived, who loved Marina with the same egoistic zeal with which a miser loves his gold, knowing the internal workings of her heart, realized how much sorrow had poured into it with the news of Yerasimos's absence, and he kept a watchful eye on her.

Straight after dinner he noticed that she had hidden fifteen white pebbles in a silver vase in her room; the same number as the days of her fiancé's absence. The next morning she took out the first and, during the course of the day, counted a dozen times the

---

22. 'Consolation'

remaining fourteen, and at dawn each day her first concern was to take out one stone. She would count the remainder, and complain that the number diminished so slowly.

Her father watched, and was tormented by her torment. On the tenth day Tapas went to her joyfully and gave her a letter from the count, and so Marina threw herself into her father's arms and kissed him fervently, overcome by spasmodic laughter mixed with tears.

In the letter, dated a week earlier, Yerasimos said that he'd arrived in Corfu two days before. However, judging from the intense feelings expressed in the rest of the letter, his mind must have been confused about the date, which couldn't be reconciled with the possibilities of wind and weather: these implied that he would have had to set out from Cephalonia three or four days earlier than when he had in fact left. But of course Marina gave less attention to the exactness of the date than she did to the letter's contents. Yerasimos, using a series of cold metaphors, said that she was the light of his eyes, the rose in the garden of his life, his rosy-lipped houri and his golden-haired angel, he assured her that without her he couldn't live, like a bird without air, like a flower without sun, that as soon as he was able to come back he would throw himself into her arms to taste the joys of paradise, and everything else he was able to translate from Italian melodrama into his own letter-writing style. In a postscript he asked the notary to tell him as soon as possible whether he had ratified the document—you know the one.

From then on Marina kept this letter in her bosom. It supported her strength and nourished her courage until the day she took the last stone from the silver vase.

She was able to get through that day, that endless day, with the help of the letter. Her anxiety since the morning was inexpressible: she wasn't able to stay in one place but went to and fro about the house, taking up and then abandoning various jobs, and only Yerasimos's letter had the power to assuage for a moment her nervous anxiety.

Towards evening her father told her he had had another letter from Yerasimos that said that his business was not yet completed and it was necessary to postpone his return for some days, he wasn't able to say how many.

'He's not coming, he's not coming,' Marina repeated, and spoke not another word all evening, except that she asked to see the letter, but in vain: the letter was in fact an invention of Tapas's to comfort her.

The next morning her father reprimanded her for her faint-heartedness; he told her that she was tempting fate in being so sad about a short absence, and urged her to be patient and sensible. Marina promised again and from then on didn't complain, but as the days passed dark circles formed round her eyes, her rosy cheeks faded, her head fell towards her breast, and she no longer sang her cheerful songs.

# IX

A month and a half had passed without Yerasimos appearing, something that didn't surprise Tapas at all, but nor had Yerasimos given any other sign of life after his first letter, and for this the notary censured him inwardly, and sometimes lied to Marina that he had heard from him.

But Marina's dull sadness continually increased, and her father, in an attempt to entertain her, took her to stay for a few days with Count Kanino in Lixouri.

Count Kanino was at that time, after Count Nannetos, the richest landowner in Cephalonia, and if at the moment he couldn't be supposed his equal in riches, it looked as if in the near future he would greatly surpass him because of his extensive business activities and his connections with important London banking houses.

His only daughter Loukia had been brought up with Marina and loved her like a sister. But they were separated by the Gulf of Argostoli, and for the young girls of Cephalonia, who were at that time still kept like charming birds in their cages, crossing the Gulf of Argostoli was no easier than crossing the Black Sea, so the two friends rarely saw each other.

So the day Marina and her father arrived was one of celebration at Count Kanino's. The two young girls, arm-in-arm all day, took walks in the lemon groves and reminisced about events of their childhood companionship, and remembered with exultation their blossoming past. But when they reached the borders of the present time, they both held back.

By confidence after confidence, the present would come in its turn, but on this first day they didn't dare touch the chord that echoed in their hearts. And in any case their shared memories were so many and varied!

After dinner and evening companionship, the two young girls retired to their bedroom. The moon was bright and shone gold on the velvet mirror of the gulf, as if the goddess Aphrodite was emerging, having washed her ambrosial hair in the liquid surface. The breeze from the gulf was refreshing, waves lapped sweetly on the shore like the whisperings of love's secrets, and the zephyr, too gentle to disturb the waters, brought on its lazy wings only the scent of the orange trees and roses, and filled all their pores with sensuality.

Loukia and Marina leant at the window hand in hand, surrendered to the enchantment of the night.

Marina was silent, and a tear appeared, welling up under her eyelids. When Loukia saw it she said, kissing her on the mouth, 'Are you melancholy, Marina?'

'This beauty, and the peace of nature,' said Marina, avoiding the question, 'exerts all its power on me and makes my heart heavy. For you, however, my lucky friend, the beauty of nature breathes gaiety. Your heart beats under the moonlight and in the scents of May like a happy nightingale. Is it then so light? Does nothing weigh on it?'

'Weigh on it?' said Loukia laughing. 'What should weigh on it? Life is so easy for us. All my days are days of May.'

'And the roses of May have no thorns?'

'Oh, if anyone dared show me their thorns,' said Loukia, laughing again, 'I would pluck them out at once.'

'But there's one that has thorns, and not so small, and it's not so easy to pluck them out. Did it never touch your happy heart?' said Marina, laying her finger on Loukia's breast.

'Ah, that's a secret, a big secret,' said Loukia, pursing her coral lips in affected seriousness.

'What secret, you cunning thing?' Marina replied. 'Didn't you tell me you have no secrets from me?'

'I did, dearest,' said Loukia, and threw herself, laughing happily, into Marina's arms. 'That's what I told you, and it shall be as I said. Only you shall know that there's someone who loves me.'

'And I wonder if he's loved by you?'

'Of course. Otherwise I wouldn't have mentioned it.'

'Well, and who is he?'

'Ah! That's the second secret. He has made my parents promise to keep the secret until my wedding day. And then, so as to avoid visits and annoyances, we're going to set out for Italy before the news is made public. If you like, that's the thorn in my rose, but I laugh about it. I hardly ever see him during the day, so sometimes I get the idea that maybe I've been tricked into marrying some changeling bat. But keep quiet about all that.'

'And has he no name?' asked Marina.

At that moment a distant melody was heard, a melody coming from the surface of the sea. At first it was hardly perceptible, like the whisper of a weak zephyr playing in the branches of a willow. But a little later it could be heard coming nearer, and the music of flute and guitar, dancing on the watery mirror, a bright and metallic sound, reached the ears of the two girls.

Loukia put her one hand to her friend's mouth, and with the other she pointed to a little boat, gliding gently on the water, looking like a black mark on the golden expanse. And indeed, soon, there rose a human voice above the instruments, singing:

*The thousand lights of heaven,*
*come out and shine with joy.*
*Modestly the moon*
*shows her lovely face.*
*Nature's thousand beauties,*
*come out and see: the stars*
*will go out when they see you;*
*the envious moon will hide.*

With the first sound of this voice, distant as it was, Marina started violently, and then all her senses were concentrated on one only, her hearing, and, forgetting where she was, forgetting Loukia who was smiling beside her, with her mouth half open she drew in a few breaths of the air that carried parts of the music and some incomprehensible syllables of the lyric.

When these first verses were finished, and guitar and flute started on the next, Loukia said, 'That's him.'

'Who?' answered Marina, as if waking suddenly with a shock from a deep sleep.

'The bat I told you about. You can hear that he doesn't have a bad voice for a bat.'

'But who is he, who is he?' said Marina, very troubled.

'Shush!' Loukia replied. 'He's starting again.'

Indeed the boat had drawn nearer, and the next verses could be heard more clearly:

*The nightingale, May's singer,*
*sings sweetly in the wood;*
*the forest wildly rustles*
*against the winds of night.*
*If just one word to utter,*
*open your rosy lips:*
*the winds of night will scatter;*
*the nightingale fall mute.*

'You can see that my roses don't have thorns,' said Loukia, laughing, when the singer stopped for a second time. 'In a week we shall marry, and hear how he's getting ready, as if he didn't have my heart already, as if he still had to win it. And for all that he's completely in agreement with my parents and with me. All the preparations have been made. Tomorrow I'll show you my dress, and the wedding crowns. But in secret: nobody must know that I showed them to you.'

'But who is he?' said Marina, as if she were talking to herself. And answering herself, 'That song, that voice…'

'Just think,' said Loukia, 'he wanted the wedding to be today. But we're not quite prepared, and my father begged him to wait until next Sunday.'

And meanwhile the boat approached nearer and nearer the open window, the oars beating gently on the waves, following the harmony of the song. The words and music of the next verses could be heard with complete clarity:

> *Clover, rose, and lily,*
> *flower, and scatter scent;*
> *earth, in the dome of heaven*
> *spills harmony and balm.*
> *You tread upon the clover*
> *with alabaster foot:*
> *the roses fade and wither;*
> *the envious lilies close.*

At that moment the boat, almost touching the shore, turned to the right to go away, and the light of the moon fell directly on the musicians and the singer.

'There, you can see him, the one who's standing up. What d'you think of my bat?'

'Count Yerasimos!' cried Marina and her cry sounded like the last sigh of one dying.

'Ah! You recognize him then?' said Loukia. 'Don't betray me: Count Yerasimos Nannetos. In a week's time I shall be Contessa Nannetos. What d'you say? Don't you approve?'

But Marina said nothing. Her face turned whiter than marble, her eyes opened wide, her teeth clamped shut spasmodically, and she fell like a stone, gasping and senseless, to the ground.

'Marina! What's the matter, sister? What's happened to you? Oh my God!' shouted Loukia, and she grasped the hands of her friend, but they were cold.

'Help! Help! Marina's fainted!' she shouted, opening the bedroom door. In the twinkling of an eye the whole household arrived.

Tapas took Marina in his arms and, as a sweat of agony broke out on his forehead, he tried to bring her round with water, massage, and smelling salts.

For half an hour all efforts proved fruitless, but eventually she sighed deeply and her body shook spasmodically. She opened her eyes and looked about her in astonishment, and with her hands brushed her curls away from her forehead:

'Thank you,' she said, smiling gently. 'It's nothing. I stayed too long at the open window, and the coldness of the sea breeze made me faint.'

'Come and calm down; sleep,' said Loukia, 'and I hope the warmth of the bed, and my care, will make you better.'

'Thank you,' replied Marina, 'but I can't. I can feel a fever in my blood. Father, please: if it's possible, it would be better for us to go home.'

Count Kanino and Loukia tried in vain to persuade her to stay at least until dawn. Tapas, uneasy about his daughter's condition, hastened to order a boat for the return to their house, in accordance with his daughter's wishes.

'Get well soon,' Loukia whispered in her ear as she left, 'and remember that you're invited to my wedding next Sunday. I want you to be there; otherwise my happiness won't be complete.'

'Well-beloved,' answered Marina, also whispering as she kissed her, 'I wish your happiness to be complete, even if I'm not there.'

When they reached Argostoli, Tapas wanted to call the doctor, but Marina said she'd recovered completely and all she needed was peace and quiet, and she retired to her room.

When she had closed the door, instead of lying down on her bed, she prostrated herself before the icon which was hanging on the wall above the bed, and having prayed for more than a quarter of an hour she got up, lit the lamp, and sat at the table to write. Her eyes were red, but dry. Her hand shook spasmodically but the force of her will supported it. She wrote as follows:

'Father, you deceived me, so that I wouldn't die of sorrow. But circumstances undermined your fatherly love's ruse. He's not in Corfu, and he won't come as he promised and as I'd been expecting for six weeks. I saw him yesterday in Lixouri. Next Sunday he's getting married to Loukia. I don't blame him: Loukia is more beautiful than I, and richer and nobler. But, forgive me, Father, I can't carry on living. I would drink any bitter cup calmly, if I knew that my black and miserable life could be a consolation to you in your old age. But no! The unbearable weight of my sorrow would be a continual torture for you. The sight of my hopelessness would be an eternal source of hopelessness for you. Let me leave for where there is rest and perhaps forgetfulness. And if you, Father, cannot forget me, then pray for me from time to time.'

Then she opened her cupboard and took out a phial of dark green liquid. Sitting on her bed, she took Yerasimos's last letter from her bosom, the letter she'd put there thirty days before, and began to read it. Her eyes, dry until now, at once welled over with tears, and about halfway through the letter she burst out sobbing. However, she carried on reading at once, and at the end, lifting her eyes to heaven, she reached for the phial with mad, spasmodic movements, brought it to her lips, and drank half the contents.

Then she lay back onto her pillow, as if exhausted by her soul's agony.

After a little while she felt some difficulty in breathing, and a few moments later she fainted. When she recovered, she felt a great tiredness in her arms and legs, and pain in the joints. She wanted to get up, but her limbs were as if broken. A cold sweat broke out over her whole body, and violent spasms started to shake it, followed by repeated faints. Then she felt great pain in her heart: she wanted to call out, but had no voice. With great effort she brought the letter she was holding to her mouth, gave a great sigh, and breathed her last.

In the morning, uneasy, her father entered her room quietly and asked in a humble voice, 'Marina, are you awake?'

Getting no answer and not wanting to disturb her he didn't go to the bed but went to the table, where his eye was caught by Marina's letter to him. He grasped it at once with a shaking hand, ran his glance over it and, beating his bald head with both hands:

'My Marina,' he shouted, 'my Marina!' and ran to the bed to embrace her.

There lay Marina, dead. Her head was arched back, pale as a withered lily, her hair, disarrayed by her agony, falling to her shoulders in chestnut curls.

In one hand she held Yerasimos's letter, in the other the death-dealing phial.

Tapas enfolded her in his embrace, kissing her all over, calling her repeatedly, tried to warm her against his chest. But in vain! The warmth of a fatherly embrace cannot melt the ice of death. Finally, Tapas realized he was tending a soulless body in vain.

Then he got up and started to go around the room like one frenzied; it was a pitiable and at the same time frightful sight, the sight of that old man. One moment he roared like a tiger whose den has been raided, the next he beat his head on the four walls of the room, the next he threatened earth and heaven with his fists, and the next he sat and wailed like a small child.

'My Marina, my daughter,' he cried, 'you've left me alone and deserted on earth. I hate and despise mankind. You were my only love, my only religion, the heart of my heart. Oh, I shall tear out the entrails of your murderer with my teeth!'

And again he started to run around like a madman.

But suddenly he started as he heard a gentle knocking at the door of the room. He looked around, and as he came to himself, he first closed the curtains of his daughter's bed, then lowered his glasses over his eyes, and opened the door to the maid, who came into the room.

'Master,' she said, 'I thought I heard you call me.'

'Yes,' answered the notary calmly, 'I called you to tell you that Marina is ill, so don't let anyone into her room. Not even yourself, unless she calls.'

And as the maid turned away he too went out, locked the door without her noticing, and took away the key.

# X

About the middle of the same day, Count Yerasimos, in Lixouri, received by the hand of an unknown boatman a letter which said as follows:

'*Carissimo* Count: I heard you'd arrived in Lixouri; welcome. I have to tell you something important concerning the business you know about. Come to my country place in Livatho at nine this evening, and knock three times on the door. I'm expecting you for dinner.'

Yerasimos paled when he read the words, 'the business you know about.'

But that evening after sunset he wrapped himself up in his cloak, crossed the harbour to Argostoli, and from there set out on foot for Livatho. The sky was cloudy and the night dark. However, he found his way to Tapas's country place with no difficulty, as he knew the road well.

When he got there he knocked three times, according to his instructions, and the notary himself answered the door. He went into the brightly lit room, which had a table set for two in the centre and against the wall a chaise longue covered with a white sheet.

'Signor Count,' said Tapas abruptly, 'welcome. So you were in Lixouri, and I didn't know.'

'Ah…' answered Yerasimos in a troubled tone, '…I had just arrived, dear Father. And I wanted to come without notice, to surprise you.'

'To surprise me! Oh, *bello*! Well, sit down, old chap. Let's eat and talk. Why are you looking round? All is well, we're alone, all alone. Even if you sounded the trumpets of Jericho, there's no one to hear you within an hour's journey from here. Sit down, I tell you.'

Yerasimos and Tapas sat at the table.

'This is a first-rate dinner,' said Yerasimos as he ate. 'This sauce is exquisite.'

'How could it be otherwise?' answered Tapas. 'I knew I had Signor Count Nannetos to receive. Well, you've sent your *povero* uncle to where there is no return. You threatened to strangle him with your own hands to get his signature, and as soon as he'd put it on the page, you smothered him with the pillows. Fabulous, by Saint Yerasimos! What d'you think of these partridges?'

'Splendid!' said Yerasimos, growing pale. 'But, Tapas old man, what sort of dinner conversation is this? Stop it, I beg you.'

'Just words to pass the time, *carissimo*. Come now! I'm sure that if you had Signor Uncle's head here, stuffed, you'd eat it to get his inheritance.'

'Tapas,' shouted Yerasimos in exasperation, pushing away the table, 'stop these jokes, otherwise I'll leave.'

'You're right; let's leave that: what's done is done and can't be undone. Come, let us drink to the health of the new Signor Count Nannetos—and to the health of his full coffers.'

Each of the two diners had a carafe of wine and a glass before him. The notary filled his own glass and drank it all down, and Yerasimos made it a point of honour not to fall behind.

'And what are you doing in Lixouri, why don't you tell me?' continued the notary.

'I told you I've only just arrived in Lixouri,' Yerasimos replied as if exasperated.

'Ah, yes! Forgive me; I forgot. But tell me, when's your wedding?'

'What wedding?' said Yerasimos in troubled tones.

'What? You've forgotten that you're going to get married? Viva the Contessa Nannetos!'

And the notary drank another glass full to the brim, Yerasimos following suit.

'How could I forget?' Yerasimos finally answered boldly. 'I didn't forget at all. But I have a few things to do and a few things to get ready in Lixouri, and in a fortnight, when I've sorted them out, I'll come to you to ask for Marina.'

'Ah! Marina!' said Tapas in a low voice like the growl of a beast. 'Let's drink one to your wedding.'

And they both emptied a third glass.

'Actually,' said the old man, 'I forgot to ask you; how does this wine seem to you?'

'It's excellent,' said Yerasimos, 'just rather strong. See, I drank it to the dregs.'

'Strange! *Curioso* thing!' said Tapas. 'And I thought poison made wine bitter.'

'What poison?'

'Ah! I forgot to tell you that too: the carafe you just drank to the dregs was half wine and half poison.'

'I don't understand what you're saying,' said Yerasimos, manifestly disturbed.

'You don't understand me, per Bacco! Come, Signor Count, and understand me: get up and pull down that sheet over there.'

Yerasimos got up from the table, still not understanding what the notary wanted to tell him, and going over to the chaise longue lifted the coverlet. But at once he gave a horrified cry and took two steps back, and the hairs on his head rose. In lifting the coverlet, he revealed the livid corpse of Marina.

'Now I'll make you understand,' said the old man in a voice like thunder. 'That was my daughter, Signor Count; that was my angel: that was my whole life. When you were a beggar and she was rich, you told her you loved her, that you'd take her for your wife, and the poor thing believed you, and forgot her father, forgot her God, and wanted only to worship you. But since you smothered your uncle and stole his life, Marina no longer seemed rich enough; you betrayed her, you left her…'

'I, my dear friend…?'

'Silence! You dare to speak! You betrayed her, I say, and on Sunday you're marrying Count Kanino's daughter. You betrayed her, and there she is! She took poison and died. Leave her there, assassino. D'you want to take her heart and eat it along with your uncle's head? She took poison, you hear? But bride and groom drink from the same cup. My daughter drank half, and died in three hours. I kept the other half and gave it to you to drink, Signor Count. In an hour you'll be as cold as crystal, in two you'll tear your flesh with your teeth, and in three hours you'll die like a dog.'

'You've poisoned me! You've poisoned me!' shouted Yerasimos, and his eyes bulged out of his head.

'Silence I say!' said Tapas, whose face had taken on an inhuman, demonic expression. 'I poisoned you, yes, but that's just one death, and if I could I'd like to give you a thousand. And so I've got this ready on your account.'

And drawing two pistols from his waist he said, grinding his teeth, 'Why are you shouting? Where are you running to, poltroon? Didn't I tell you there's no one to hear you within an hour of here? It's no use pulling at that door, it's locked, and I've got the key.'

'Tapas, in the name of God, in the name of all you love in the world…!' shouted Yerasimos, shaking like a leaf.

'All I love in the world! Blackguard! All I love in the world is there, dead, and you killed her for me.'

'Tapas, my dear Tapas, show some compassion!'

'Pray, I tell you, to the devil to come and carry away your soul. Let me try this pistol, to see if it shoots straight.'

And he shot his victim at three paces. Yerasimos, hands up, fell dead on the floor.

'Pretty good,' said the notary with an infernal laugh, 'for a hand that's seen seventy summers. And should I leave the other pistol dissatisfied? Perhaps the dog hasn't lost his soul yet, and might feel the pain of a third death.'

And with cold-blooded beastliness he emptied the second pistol in him.

Then, approaching Marina's dead body, he kissed her on the forehead.

'My daughter, I didn't deceive you,' he said, 'I promised you I'd give you your man. There he is: I gave him to you.'

Then he took the key from his pocket, opened the door, went outside and set off towards the town.

The night around him was black as pitch. Things could be made out vaguely and uncertainly: the trees seemed like gigantic corpses waving their dead arms up and down, and the wind raging among them was like the wailing of the dead.

In a quarter of an hour he met his servant under a big tree, who was waiting for him with his horse readied.

The notary gave the servant a thick letter and said to him, 'For the Avocato Fiscale. To be in his hands before dawn.'

And once the servant had set out for Argostoli, the notary mounted the horse, turned his back on the town, and receded into the distance at a gallop.

# XI

The day of Rodini's execution arrived, and before sunrise the condemned man had already risen from his straw bed. Standing at the window of his cell he awaited the arrival of the light, and when he saw the sun rise above the hills, he greeted it, and whispered,

'For the last time.'

Then he turned his loving gaze to the plain, the mountain, the sea; to everything that was within the range of his sight. Finally he turned his eyes to the heavens, to which his heart rose on the wings of prayer.

At that moment the iron door of his cell could be heard creaking on its hinges, and Rodini turned to see the turnkey on the threshold, and behind him someone with a harsh gaze and revolting appearance.

'The time has come?' asked Rodini.

'It has come,' answered the turnkey. 'The sun has risen.'

'And how beautifully it rose,' answered Rodini. 'Did no one ask to see me this morning?'

'Yes indeed,' answered the turnkey, 'but they were ordered to wait below. If you are ready, let us go down.'

'Ready...' said Rodini. 'Yes, I am.'

And handing him a ring, he added:

'But before we go down, take this as a memento of the kindness you showed me, though you were my guard.'

Then the old turnkey warmly took Rodini's hand and brought it to his lips.

'Mr Rodini,' he said, 'even if this hand were to give me millions, I should not bring it to my lips if I thought it had murdered.'

'Thank you, my friend,' said Rodini. 'The confidence of a heart such as yours is the greatest consolation in these moments.'

Then he turned to the man who had come with the turnkey, the executioner, and said to him:

'I believe my clothes belong to you by law. In my pockets you will find my wallet, which contains the compensation for your efforts. It is not your fault that those efforts are not pleasing to me.'

And he saw the executioner come forward holding a rope in his hands.

'What do you want?' asked Rodini calmly.

'I must...' he answered, trying to soften the harshness of his voice, 'with your permission, I must tie your hands.'

'I am in no position to refuse,' answered Rodini with a bitter smile. 'Do what you are required to do.'

But the turnkey stopped him.

'Leave him, leave him,' he said. 'You have time to do it when you get there.'

And thus they went down the steps from the cell. But at the gates of the yard Rodini stopped short, troubled, because before the threshold he met Angeliki, or rather the ghost of Angeliki, who was unable to stand on her own feet and was supported on one side by her father and on the other by old Nikola, the deceased count's servant, both of whom were weeping.

But when she saw him approaching, Angeliki, as if all the dormant springs of her life were stretched at once, threw herself upon him, hung with both hands on his shoulder, and started to cry loudly. At the same time, both Voratis and Nikola took his two hands and they, too, wetted them with their tears.

Rodini squeezed their hands with all the ardour that his immense gratitude to them had provoked, and with his arm supported Angeliki, who was in danger of falling to the ground again. Thus began his last journey, and, walking to his death, he carried his half-dead fiancée and comforted and encouraged her with his words:

'What are you afraid of?' he said, 'For me? For my bodily pain? One moment of agony. You are afraid of our temporary separation? Eternity shall be ours. If our bridal crowns wither when hardly woven, in heaven the martyr's crown of stars awaits us. Don't talk or think of hopelessness. Hope flowers on the stem of virtue. Do not hurry to leave life until your Creator calls you, and then, be assured that our souls will be reunited in His bosom.'

'Our souls are one soul,' whispered Angeliki, weeping heart-rendingly. 'They want to fly to heaven together. Mine waits on the edge of my lips. Two fates weigh on the consciences of your judges.'

Thus they arrived at the frightful place where the condemned were executed by hanging, and where the bodies remained hanging for many days, playthings of the winds and prey to the birds, for all to see as fearful examples.

In the middle of the square rose the abominable gibbet, and next to it, in a great cauldron over a big fire, pitch was boiling, used to preserve the bodies of the hanged so that they could bear the many days of exhibition on the gallows.

Few condemned men walked to their deaths like Rodini, accompanied by friends and relatives as if going to a celebration, because of course few who had been condemned to a dishonourable death failed to provoke shame in their friends and relations.

And when he reached the gallows, the executioner approached again to tie his hands.

'One moment, please,' said Rodini, and taking from his bosom the will he had written and sealed the previous night, he gave it to Voratis.

'I appoint you,' he said, 'executor of my will. When I am dead, open it, and do as I order.'

Then, when he had kissed in succession Voratis, Nikolos and Angeliki:

'I thank you,' he said, 'that you gave me this final and public demonstration of your faithfulness; accompanying me and accepting my embrace. And if God does not recognize the inward workings of hearts, this testimony in my favour would suffice for him.'

Then he said to the executioner:

'Now I'm ready.'

But Voratis again threw himself into his arms and said:

'Go where the angels of heaven await you, and pray there for us who remain behind to weep for a little while longer, and then to follow you.'

Nikolos too embraced him and wanted to speak, but his tears drowned his voice completely.

Finally Angeliki, who embraced him as a mother embraces her child to protect him from imminent danger, would not be separated from him, for all that the executioner approached twice.

'No,' she said, 'you shall not raise your hand against the innocent. If you want a victim, come, take me. You shall not draw near him.'

But the officer who was responsible for the execution, approaching Voratis, begged him to pull his daughter away and to point out to her that it was unbecoming for a noble young woman to behave in such a manner before the gaze of the public.

Angeliki heard this.

'Unbecoming!' she shouted, forgetting her natural modesty. 'You murder him, and you talk of what is unbecoming! It's not a joke, it's the terrible truth. You are going to murder him! No, you won't kill him unless you kill me first.'

'If she doesn't keep her distance,' said the officer, speaking again to Voratis, 'then I'm sorry, but I shall be obliged to order two soldiers to take her away.'

Then Rodini gave the officer an indignant look, and, having kissed Angeliki for the last time on the forehead, said:

'Farewell!' and he pushed her away himself, while her father and Nikolos combined their efforts in taking her away.

At the same moment the executioner cut the scene short by approaching Rodini, with the deadly noose in his hands, and asked him to lower his head.

But at that very moment a distant, agonised shout could be heard:

'Stop! Stop!'

And the public prosecutor appeared, running into the execution yard.

'In the name of God, stop!' he said again, gasping as he arrived, waving some papers he had in his hand.

'What's happening? What's going on?' a thousand voices asked as one, and the officers and the first of all those present surrounded him.

'Stop!' he called again, as if afraid they hadn't understood. 'Rodini is to be freed: Rodini is innocent.'

And showing the officers the order of the chief justice, he demanded that the condemned be handed over.

The officer hastened, without bringing any objection, to obey the order, and Rodini grasped the hand of the public prosecutor and, opening his arms wide, closed into one embrace his future father-in-law, the faithful servant, and Angeliki, who was supported by the other two. Voratis kissed Rodini passionately on the head:

'You are given back to us, my son,' he said. 'So justice is done on earth.'

Old Nikolos fell to his knees and crossed himself three times, saying formally:

'Great art thou, Lord, and wondrous thy works.'

But Angeliki was overcome by such persistent spasms of wailing that she had to be taken home, where she remained ill in bed for many days.

And all the surrounding crowd, even if they didn't know the reason, cheered and clapped, because, however much the love of the Cephalonians for the murdered old man had provoked very deep anger against his suspected and, as they had thought, proven murderer, they all loved and respected Rodini too, so it was with great joy that they heard that he was innocent.

Of course, the public prosecutor led his prisoner directly to the court, where the judges, previously advised of this turn of events, were gathered in exceptional conference. There, he said:

'Gentlemen of the court, only the all-wise God is infallible. Only his eyes see, always and everywhere, the truth. The judgement of man is fallible. It is, however, our duty, when the truth appears through the mist, to declare it in a loud voice. I prevented the execution of sentence on Mr Rodini, as I have the right to do with the permission of the chairman of the court, because new evidence has been revealed that shows the conviction was not correct, and I don't wish, as you, too, certainly don't wish, the blood of the innocent to be on our hands and those of our children.'

Following this prologue, which caused astonishment in the court, he read a letter addressed to himself from the notary Tapas, written in Italian, the translation of which is as follows:

*To the Public Prosecutor:*

*The evidence I gave in court concerning the death of Count Nannetos was false. The count's will in favour of Rodini is the only genuine one. The other, in favour of his nephew Yerasimos, is a fake. I faked it, in collusion with Yerasimos, because he had promised he would marry my daughter. As proof, let my ledger of transactions be examined, where this will is not noted, nor is the count's signature in the ledger, as the rules require. Yerasimos, having a spare key to his uncle's house, entered by night, threatened the count with murder and forced him to sign the false will. Then, so that the count could not betray him, he smothered him with the pillows of his bed. I enclose a letter from Yerasimos, in which he had the naivety to confide in writing what he had done. Do not vainly seek the murderer, or if you seek him, go to my establishment in Livatho. There you will find only his body.*

*I shall anticipate the justice of God and the hangman's noose: in an hour from now I shall have poisoned him with the wine from my dinner table, and I shall smash his head with a bullet from my own weapon, because he deceived my daughter, and he killed her with his betrayal. There you will find her too, the ill-fated one, dead: give her a Christian burial. She is an innocent victim. Do not look for me; by the time you get this letter, I shall not be in Cephalonia.*

After he had read it aloud, the prosecutor handed the letter and Yerasimos's enclosure to the presiding judge of the court and, as his only conclusion and epilogue, added, 'I request the release of Rodini.'

The court retired to consider, and when they returned a little later announced that they found Rodini innocent and fit to be released, but that he must remain confined until the revocation of the court's earlier decision could be sought from and ratified by the high commissioner.

Meanwhile, the police went to the notary's country house in Livatho. In the main room they found the table still set, and on it the remains of the dinner: at one side of the table, in a pool of blood, was the mutilated body of Yerasimos, and on the other side, on the chaise longue, the dead Marina, dressed as a bride, with her hands crossed on her chest, and a wreath of flowers on her head.

The court, believing that justice must be done completely, judged Yerasimos, for all that he was dead, and found him guilty of forgery and parricide. His body was brought to the place of execution, soaked in stinking pitch and hanged on the gallows, where it remained for a month, to be swayed by the winds; a fearful sight for the inhabitants of Argostoli who, as they passed, would turn their gaze away and cross themselves.

Marina was given burial with due ceremony, because the fact that she had poisoned herself did not become known. The whole town accompanied the coffin of the young and beautiful girl to her last resting place, and wept for the victim of the evildoer. Among the others, Loukia, the daughter of Count Kanino, came too, dressed in black: she always wore black from that day forth because she retired to spend the rest of her life in a nunnery.

Rodini's house arrest was more for the sake of appearances than reality, so it was enforced with much leniency, and by his own choice it took place in Voratis's house, where Angeliki's illness kept him voluntarily confined far more severely than the law.

The confirmation of his innocence presented no difficulty by reason of the special circumstances of the case, and was officially announced on the same day that Angeliki recovered. Their marriage took place without delay, and immediately after the service the newly married couple, accompanied by Voratis, left Cephalonia—a place of sad and repugnant memories for them—forever, and they settled in one of the European commercial towns, where Rodini became one of the best and most widely respected merchants.

# XII

Everyone remembers, during the first years of the Greek Revolution, an old Ionian Islander dressed in rags, who wandered around the towns and the army camps carrying his possessions on his shoulders. Sewn on to his stinking rags, before and behind, he had birds' feathers, dogs' tails, and other grotesque things, which made the children laugh. He became the plaything of the soldiers everywhere; they would laugh at his obscene gestures and his nonsensical talk, and reward him with bones thrown from their tables. Sometimes his madness would reach a peak of mania, mainly when he happened to see blood. Then, meaningless talk would spill from his mouth.

'Well done, Count, my boy,' he could be heard saying. 'Squeeze, squeeze tight, until the old man bursts. Look at him! The *povero*, his eyes are bulging! Suck them out, before they pop out at you. Oh, you son of a bitch! You slaughtered my white dove! Ah, *bestia!*[23] You gave my sweet lamb poison to drink! Drink, Yerasimos, drink to the health of the devil! Uncle's paying! A fire burns my hands, Yerasimos, and my tongue! I'd like to wash my hands in your blood! I'd like to suck your brains out to quench my thirst!'

His face took on a bestial expression when he pronounced these infernal fantasies, but the boorish soldiers laughed as they heard him, and they incited him to repeat them, even though they knew that, when the frightful crisis was over, he would go away enraged and not reappear for two days.

This wretched beggar was Tapas the notary. Not having the courage to bear, in his own land, the punishment for what he'd done—death by hanging—that terrible night of Yerasimos's murder he'd escaped to Greece, simply changing his name slightly. In Greece now, feeling himself hammered by the fates and drowning his reason in bloody fantasies and sorrow for the loss of his daughter, he had been reduced to such a pitiable state that he was a fearful example of God's justice, and a reiteration of Cain's punishment.

Indeed, when after the fall of Missolonghi to the Turks, the warlord Karaïskakis led a campaign in Mainland Greece to take revenge for that martyred city, the old Cephalonian found himself among the

---

23. 'Beast!'

army camp's beasts of burden. And he happened to follow a group of soldiers which, forced by the fate of war, was headed towards the shore.

It was approaching sunset when, after one of his frequent explosions of mania, he went out, maddened, from the camp, and started to wander aimlessly among the mountains. He climbed as quickly as a wild cat up a rocky slope which rose in front of him, and found himself on the edge of a precipice, the base of which—more than 200 feet below—was grinding under the continually breaking waves. Tapas gazed over the Ionian Sea and saw on the brightly lit western horizon Cephalonia showing clearly opposite him, and his heart leapt as if it would break as he made out, there before him, the familiar shape of the peak of Mount Ainos.

'Marina, my Marina!' he cried. 'I ran all over the world looking for you; I ran night and day, in valleys and on mountains. There you were, my daughter, waiting for me! Don't go away; I'm coming, I'm coming!'

And he took one pace towards the vision of his heart. But that pace was over the precipice. And the foaming waves extinguished the pangs of his conscience, and his pains, and his memory.

# Endnote

\* *The Notary* was published in 1855, a few years before the unification of the Ionian Islands with the newly established modern Greek state. Rangavis on several occasions makes reference to the Italian linguistic and cultural inheritance of the islands, especially to the use of Italian as the official language of legal and bureaucratic affairs. The following is an instance that has been cut from the text for the contemporary reader:

> His speech was, as unfortunately throughout the Ionian Islands at that time, a bastardised monstrosity of mixed Greek and Italian. And I say that not in any spirit of irony, but rather in commiseration with my fellow islanders. Under the Venetian dynasty, the noblest sign of our national identity was in danger of being lost; the voice of Homer forgotten by the sons of Odysseus. At the same time, however, I want commend them for their brave and successful efforts to improve their use of the national language, and in this they have many champions.

# Biographical Note

1809    Alexandros Rizos Rangavis born in Constantinople on the 27th of December. His mother was Zoe Lapithi, daughter of Efstathios Lapithi from Zagora in Pelion, a well-off dealer of precious stones. His father was Iakovos Rizos Rangavis.

1813    When their house was destroyed by fire, the family left Constantinople and went to Bucharest, where they stayed until 1821 in the court of Vlachia's ruler, Alexandros Soutsos, who was Iakovos Rangavis's uncle. While there, Alexandros came in contact with European literature.

1821    When the Greek War of Independence broke out, the Rangavis family, expelled by the Turks, took refuge in Stephanopolis in Romania. There, Alexandros became a pupil in a Greek school.

1822    In spring, the family moved to Odessa. For a while they stayed in the house of Maria Soutsos, the sister of Rangavis's mother. Alexandros studied at home under the tutelage of Georgios Yennadios, then went to the Greek Commercial School of Odessa.

1825    Rangavis travelled to Munich where, with a scholarship from King Ludwig of Bavaria, he studied at the Military Academy. Took lessons with Schelling and Tirs, and was by this point already fluent in two or three foreign languages.

1829  Moved to Nafplio, the first capital of Greece, on the 2nd of January and enlisted in the military as an artillery sub-lieutenant.

1830  Left military service to devote himself to politics, philology and archaeology.

1831  First literary publication, the extended narrative poem 'Demos and Eleni', written in the style of the demotic song and in a language close to the demotic (Kathomiloumeni) version of Greek. In this period he also wrote many patriotic poems, inspired by the Greek Revolution, in the same demotic style.

1831–32  Visited Athens for the first time that winter, as part of the government committee concerned with the addition of Attica and Evia to the newly established state of Greece.

1832  Appointed to the council of the Ministry of Education. Responsible for the establishment of the University of Athens which would open the following year; also for the organization of middle and higher education.

1834  Moved to Athens, the new capital of Greece, at the beginning of December. Published, with Constantinos Pop and Ioannis Deliyannis, the first Greek literary periodical, *Iris*.

1837  Published his first prose piece under the title 'Prisons and Capital Punishment'. His prologue to the dramatic work *Phrosini* became a manifesto of romanticism in Greece.

1839   Married the English woman Caroline Skean.

1844   On the 11th of November, Rangavis was appointed as regular lecturer in archaeology at the University of Athens, where he would stay until 1867. During this period, he taught four basic subjects: archaeology, history of Ancient Greek art, epigraphy and ancient politics.

1845   Under the pseudonym Christophanos Neologidis, published the play *Koutroulis's Marriage*, a political comedy which was later translated into German.

1847   In September, with his old classmate Grigoris Kampouroglou, founded a new chiefly literary periodical, *Euterpi*. (1847–55).

1849   With the cooperation of N. Dragoumis and K. Paparigopoulos, started a new scientific and literary periodical, *Pandora*. In the following years many of his stories would be published here, as well as his historical novel *The Chief of Morea* and the novella *The Notary*.

1850   On the 8th of September, was awarded honorary membership of the London Philological Society.

1855   Organized archaeological excavations at Eraios in Argos. In the same year, he was chosen as an Athens Town Councillor.

1856–59   Appointed Foreign Minister. During this period he oversaw the founding of the Zappeion Hall and the National Orphanage, and among other important works, the building of the Athens Observatory.

1866    Appointed Dean of Athens University. Published his *History of Ancient Art* and the verse drama *The Thirty Tyrants*.

1867–87    Appointed Ambassador to the United States of America, Constantinople, Paris and Berlin.

1877    His *History of Modern Greek Literature* is published in French. It was the first attempt at a record of Greek literary production.

1882    His *History of Modern Greek Literature* is published in German.

1892    Died in January in Athens, at the age of 83.

CORFU

Corfu Town

MAINLAND
GREECE

PAXOS

*Ionian Sea*

LEFKAS

ACARNANIA

ITHAKA

CEPHALONIA

Missolonghi

Lixouri · Argostoli

PELOPONNESE

ZANTE

MAP OF THE IONIAN ISLANDS

MODERN
GREEK
CLASSICS

www.aiorabooks.com

**C.P. CAVAFY**
## Selected Poems
Translated by David Connolly

Cavafy is by far the most translated and well-known Greek poet internationally. Whether his subject matter is historical, philosophical or sensual, Cavafy's unique poetic voice is always recognizable by its ironical, suave, witty and world-weary tones.

**ODYSSEUS ELYTIS**
1979 NOBEL PRIZE FOR LITERATURE
## In the Name of Luminosity and Transparency
With an Introduction by Dimitris Daskalopoulos

The poetry of Odysseus Elytis owes as much to the ancients and Byzantium as to the surrealists of the 1930s and the architecture of the Cyclades, bringing romantic modernism and structural experimentation to Greece. Collected here are the two speeches Elytis gave on his acceptance of the 1979 Nobel Prize for Literature.

NIKOS ENGONOPOULOS
## Cafés and Comets After Midnight
## and Other Poems
BILINGUAL EDITION
Translated by David Connolly

Derided and maligned for his innovative and, at the time, often incomprehensible modernist experiments, Engonopoulos is today regarded as one of the most original artists of his generation and as a unique figure in Greek letters. In both his painting and poetry, he created a peculiarly Greek surrealism, a blending of the Dionysian and Apollonian.

M. KARAGATSIS
## The Great Chimera
Translated by Patricia Barbeito

A psychological portrait of a young French woman, Marina, who marries a sailor and moves to the island of Syros, where she lives with her mother-in-law and becomes acquainted with the Greek way of life. Her fate grows entwined with that of the boats and when economic downturn arrives, it brings passion, life and death in its wake.

STELIOS KOULOGLOU
## Never Go to the Post Office Alone
Translated by Joshua Barley

A foreign correspondent in Moscow queues at the city's central post office one morning in 1989, waiting to send a fax to his newspaper in New York. With the Soviet Union collapsing and the Berlin Wall about to fall, this moment of history would change the world, and his life, forever.

ANDREAS LASKARATOS
## Reflections
BILINGUAL EDITION
Translated by Simon Darragh
With an Introduction by Yorgos Y. Alisandratos

Andreas Laskaratos was a writer and poet, a social thinker and, in many ways, a controversialist. His *Reflections* sets out, in a series of calm, clear and pithy aphorisms, his uncompromising and finely reasoned beliefs on morality, justice, personal conduct, power, tradition, religion and government.

MARGARITA LIBERAKI
## The Other Alexander
Translated by Willis Barnstone and Elli Tzalopoulou

First published in the 1950s to international acclaim, Margarita Liberaki's allegorical novel, *The Other Alexander*, speaks to the opposing forces inherent in human nature. This exquisite poetic drama reenacts Greek tragedy in its evocation of a country riven by civil war and a family divided against itself.

ALEXANDROS PAPADIAMANDIS
## Fey Folk
Translated by David Connolly

Alexandros Papadiamandis holds a special place in the history of Modern Greek letters, but also in the heart of the ordinary reader. *Fey Folk* follows the humble lives of quaint, simple-hearted folk living in accordance with centuries-old traditions and customs, described here with both reverence and humour.

EMMANUEL ROÏDES
## Pope Joan
Translated by David Connolly

Roïdes' irreverent, witty and delightful novel tells the story of Joan who, according to a popular medieval legend, ascended to the Papal Throne as Pope John VIII. In Joan, Roïdes has created one of the most remarkable characters in modern Greek literature and in so doing has assured his place as one of its classic authors.

ANTONIS SAMARAKIS
## The Flaw
Translated by Simon Darragh

A man is seized from his afternoon drink at the Cafe Sport by two agents of the Regime by car toward Special Branch Headquarters, and the interrogation that undoubtedly awaits him there. Part thriller and part political satire, *The Flaw* has been translated into more than thirty languages.

GEORGE SEFERIS
1963 NOBEL PRIZE FOR LITERATURE
## Novel and Other Poems          BILINGUAL EDITION
Translated by Roderick Beaton

Often compared during his lifetime to T.S. Eliot, George Seferis is noted for his spare, laconic, dense and allusive verse in the Modernist idiom of the first half of the twentieth century. Seferis better than any other writer expresses the dilemma experienced by his countrymen then and now: how to be at once Greek and modern.

MAKIS TSITAS
**God Is My Witness**
Translated by Joshua Barley

A hilariously funny and achingly sad portrait of Greek society during the crisis years, as told by a lovable anti-hero. Fifty-year-old Chrysovalantis, who has recently lost his job and struggles with declining health, sets out to tell the story of his life, roaming the streets of Athens on Christmas Eve with nothing but a suitcase in hand.

ILIAS VENEZIS
**Serenity**
Translated by Joshua Barley

Inspired by the author's own experience of migration, the novel follows the journey of a group of Greek refugees from Asia Minor who settle in a village near Athens. It details the hatred of war, the love of nature that surrounds them, the hostility of their new neighbours and eventually their adaptation to a new life.

GEORGIOS VIZYENOS
**Thracian Tales**
Translated by Peter Mackridge

These short stories bring to life Vizyenos' native Thrace, a corner of Europe where Greece, Turkey and Bulgaria meet. Through masterful psychological portayals, each story keeps the reader in suspense to the very end: Where did Yorgis' grandfather travel on his only journey? What was Yorgis' mother's sin? Who was responsible for his brother's murder?

**GEORGIOS VIZYENOS**
## Moskov Selim
Translated by Peter Mackridge

A novella by Georgios Vizyenos, one of Greece's best-loved writers, set in Thrace during the time of the Russo-Turkish War, whose outcome would decide the future of southeastern Europe. *Moskov Selim* is a moving tale of kinship, despite the gulf of nationality and religion.

**NIKIFOROS VRETTAKOS**
## Selected Poems                    BILINGUAL EDITION
Translated by David Connolly

The poems of Vrettakos are firmly rooted in the Greek landscape and coloured by the Greek light, yet their themes and sentiment are ecumenical. His poetry offers a vision of the paradise that the world could be, but it is also imbued with a deep and painful awareness of the dark abyss that the world threatens to become.

**AN ANTHOLOGY**
## Rebetika: Songs from
## the Old Greek Underworld        BILINGUAL EDITION
Edited and translated
by Katharine Butterworth and Sara Schneider

The songs in this book are a sampling of the urban folk songs of Greece during the first half of the twentieth century. Often compared to American blues, rebetika songs are the creative expression of the *rebetes*, people living a marginal and often underworld existence on the fringes of established society.

AN ANTHOLOGY
## Greek Folk Songs
BILINGUAL EDITION

Translated by Joshua Barley

The Greek folk songs were passed down from generation
to generation in a centuries-long oral tradition, lasting
until the present. Written down at the start of the nineteenth century, they became the first works of modern
Greek poetry, playing an important role in forming the
country's modern language and literature.